Praise for *Ho*

"Rhythmic, visceral, laconic, powerful, Levy's stories will haunt the reader long after reading them."
- Nguyen Ba Chung, *William Joiner Center*

"...I was excited to read *How Stevie Nearly Lost the War*, and I was not disappointed. Any family member, any therapist, who wants to know something of the pain that vets carry in their heads and hearts...should read this book."
- Hamilton Gregory, *MacNamara's Folly*

"Here is a fine collection by one of the Vietnam War's finest writers. His quiet voice details a variety of experience hard to come by. The stories click with a kind of muted rage, a majestic astonishment, the fine appreciation of deep irony, and unmistakable authority. Buy this book, and learn a thing or two about the war that defined and baffled and energized a generation."
- Larry Heineman, *Paco's Story*, recipient of the *National Book Award*

"Some of the most eloquent voices in the history of American war literature have come out of the tragedy of the American War in Vietnam. Enter Marc Levy, a dazzling stylist, who takes readers on a wild ride in this perfectly paced collection of stories. Funny and furious, his characters, with all their injuries, love and live to the hilt. *How Stevie Nearly Lost the War* is hard to put down. Levy is a master storyteller. This book will last."
- Demetria Martinez, *Mother Tongue*

"His writing is about the aftermath that follows you home. His words flow like poetry, exposing the carnage and madness of war."
- Frank Serpico

"Levy got me with his first sentence – 'Anyone can say they were in Vietnam.' I pay his work the ultimate compliment that I pay Tim O'Brien's *The Things They Carried* – the lines between fact and fiction are blurred, and that, my friends, is exactly what Vietnam was like. Read this collection."
- Doug Rawlings, co-founder, *Veterans for Peace*

"In these days when those with power over our fate are working overtime to obliterate truth and memory, Marc Levy's brutal honesty and authenticity are just what we need. His new volume of stories will not let you forget the reality of Vietnam and of war."
- H. Bruce Franklin, *Vietnam and Other American Fantasies*

"It is the most powerful report I know about the post war experience. The overall character of Levy's time as an Army medic comes through in passages like this: 'At first I never killed anyone. The machine gunners and riflemen did that. I carried morphine and bandages to ease their pain. Then I helped in the killing. And the killing helped me.' Read this book, and if you ever again find yourself wishing to volunteer for service abroad in the US military, I'll be surprised."
- Staughton Lynd, co author, *Moral Injury and Nonviolent Resistance*

"Levy has collected some of his best short stories in a small but powerful book about life and death with the 1st Air Cavalry Division in Vietnam and his endless attempts since

to describe, remember and deal with the memories and pain he still packs with him. 'Wherever you were, whatever you did in war will always be with you,' he tells younger vets. 'Always.' "
        - Michael Putzel, *The Price They Paid: Enduring Wounds of War*

"In the words of his alter-ego in *How Stevie Nearly Lost the War*, Marc Levy writes with 'the unerring chaos, the unpredictable beat, the cyclic consequences, the sorrow of war.' His prose breaks all bounds of fiction and non-fiction with exhilarating zeal. Get ready for a wild ride."
        - Dave Zieger, director of *Sir, No Sir!*

"These stories pull no punches. Something good or strange is always just around the corner. The best of them bring the war home — its casualties are tragic and frightening, yet almost hopeful in all their sorrow."
        - Paul Krassner, *Confessions of a Raving, Unconfined Nut*

"A bold and troubling, surreal, rambling account of a Vietnam veteran's struggles with PTSD and memories. A former combat medic, Levy's travels and traumas in search of human kindness and understanding offer grim testimony to the aftereffects of war."
        - John Ketwig,
        ...and a hard rain fell: A G.I.'s True Story of the War in Vietnam

How Stevie Nearly Lost the War
and Other Postwar Stories

Marc Levy

4 Nov 17

To Joe,

with best regards,
Marc Levy

Winter Street Press
Salem, MA 01970

How Stevie Nearly Lost the War and Other Postwar Stories

ISBN: 978-0-692-77638-4

First Edition

Cover photo: detail from a Greek amphora (circa 525 BC) depicting Achilles and Ajax playing a dice game.

For Erin

Acknowledgments

I would like to thank the following persons for their encouragement and editorial advice: George Dickerson, Susan Moger, Richard Levine, Erin McManus, Larry Heinemann, Bruce Weigl, Martha Collins, Nancy Esposito, Jennifer Belle, and Jill Hoffman.

Contents

"War is sweet to those who do not know it."

Pindar

How Stevie Nearly Lost the War
and Other Postwar Stories

Speak Out

Anyone can say they were in Vietnam. Anyone can say I was a medic humping the boonies, did two, three tours, got shot at, plugged guys with bandages and morphine to ease the pain. Anyone can say they were in Vietnam. But not me. I'd never do that. I'm the genuine article. The real deal. I have the papers and medals to prove it.

At a warehouse in Secaucus, NJ surrounded by electrified chain linked fence, armed guards with six-legged pit bulls who speak in tongues guard over my hundred thousand medals of honor. On Tuesdays I charge three dollars for the radical walking tour.

I've been awarded the Distinguished Service Cross so many times the Army sent me a telegram in 1978:

SIR, PLEASE BE ADVISED WE HAVE RUN OUT OF SHEET METAL AND RIBBON FABRIC. THE JOINT CHIEFS OF STAFF HAVE COMMISSIONED A TEAM TO SCULPT YOUR LIKENESS ON MT. RUSHMORE. CONGRATULATIONS AND GOD BLESS THE UNITED STATES OF AMERICA.

The Silver Star is the third highest decoration for gallantry in combat. I keep all 2,000 one for every citizen in Dentville, Wisconsin in six hundred solid oak treasure chests. When the moon is full, I lift the lid of one such chest, sink my hand deep into the glistening pile, hurl them high with all my

1

strength. When the tinkling stars shower down, winking, it reminds me of the Milky Way.

Do not doubt me. You have my word all this is terribly true. I was no ordinary medic during those dim days of yesteryear. No, sir. No, mam.

I performed brain surgery in the dark, twelve men at a time without benefit of anesthetic to obtain the element of surprise. I called in B-52 strikes using my sinus cavities to broadcast outgoing signals. I was born in a bomb crater on the third of July.

In my pack I carried entire battalions of tanks and cannons. The blades of helicopters poked out from beneath my helmet. Snagged on clouds, slowed me down. I fired my M-16 eighty-two trillion times. It never once jammed or malfunctioned.

I dug five hundred million foxholes. I ate nine billion cans of C-rations. I drank thirty-nine hundred million gallons of water. I defecated six hundred sixty-six million metric tons of highly enriched government issued poo. A not immodest sum don't you think?

Anyone can say they were in Vietnam. But I'm the real deal, the genuine article. I have the papers and medals to prove it. You meet me 2:30 in the afternoon in Secaucus, NJ I'll give you the tour. But those under eighteen will not be admitted.

How Stevie Nearly Lost The War

The war, Stevie is told, with its white-tailed rockets and hard crack ricochets; the war, with its thumping whirl of trembling choppers; the war, with its shirtless gun crews manning steel wheeled cannons; the war, with its fine plumed shells cutting silver arcs through infinite sky; the war, with its lumbering tanks and sun bleached bunkers; the war, with its steep, lush highlands, emerald lattice of checkerboard paddies; the war, with its mangled torsos triaged too late; the war, he is told on scheduled clinic days, had ended quite some time ago.

Stevie sits on the bare floor in the center of his nine by nine studio apartment; it is a good thing to do. Long past midnight, seated cross-legged, facing the solitary open window opposite his computer and metal file cabinet, he leans against his white book case and recalls the soft patter of rain on tropical wood, the curling trickle of thin, incessant rivulets. In tropical forests before first light, all sound felt amplified, organic. Yet nothing happened; nothing of consequence.

Years later, he regretted that while angry young men wearing torn battle fatigues, unit patches, mud-slicked boonie hats, hurled their combat medals onto capitol steps–some weeping, other's shouting, yet strangely peaceful in their rude dissent–Stevie lay snug beneath an olive-drab stockade blanket, thin, exhausted, hair close cut, unable to attend.

Soon he will rise to make toast, the preferred meal of day or night. For now, Stevie thinks of Cindy's last letter, and Cindy herself. She is short, of medium build, with auburn hair and alluring, firm calves. Of particular note is the manner in which her mouth seems to push forward, as though a permanent kiss strained her curious face. She is pretty, but not in the conventional sense. He had known her in passing, knew his curious manner did not unnerve her. She read well in public. Her writing was better than most encountered at café readings. When Stevie read about war, not once in two years did Cindy look away. Stevie remembers their only date.

"Would you like to go out sometime?"

"Sure," she said.

The very next afternoon they walked for hours in the lush wood of a nearby state park. Toward evening, they returned to Cindy's well-kept house.

"You can come in. I trust you," she said.

Her home was filled with fine antique furniture exquisitely placed. The walls were earth toned, adorned with Audubon prints. The carpeting was soft and thick, rich with patterns of amber and blue. They sat on a plush white love seat.

"This is Sasha," Cindy beamed.

Stevie gently stroked the calm, beige cat behind its scarred left ear. When the trustful creature tired of his touch, it jumped from his lap and scurried away. Then Stevie kissed Cindy. Simply kissed her full on the mouth. His tongue wandered, his fingertips traveled beneath her red silk sweater. She pulled him, pressed herself tight against his torso, then murmured, "Do you want to?"

And Stevie said, "No."

(Because he did not wish to fuck her like Bride would have. Sharing a foxhole, Bride regaled Stevie with prodigious stories of sexual conquest. Seventy women. Found. Fucked. Forgotten. Then a single shot rang out and the burly sergeant slumped forward, dark blood gathering beneath his head. When the sniper was caught the platoon butchered her. Stevie held her down).

"It won't work, Cindy. We'll end up hating each other. I know it," he said.

He never spoke this way: polite, casual, comforting.

"What do you want?" she said, straightening her clothes. She was lovely, he thought. So lovely.

"Just be my friend. Will you be my friend?"

When Cindy said "Yes" Stevie wept susurrant tears.

"Why are you crying, Stevie?"

"I don't know," he said. "I don't know."

She held him close until his time came to leave.

In one seamless arc Stevie rises and seats himself at his computer, a mongrel stitched from the wreckage of other people's lives. It is late. The perfect time to write Cindy, who must be sleeping.

Subject: Memo Day
Date: Tuesday 30 May 2001 3am
From: Silverspartan
To: Mimsypearl

The Memorial Day service went well. They played the Billy Joel song with chopper blades in the background. No caffeine in your blood, that'll wake you up. Old men read poems about duty, honor, that sort of thing. The crowd loved it. Then it's my turn. I tell them things they need to hear. A few vets said, "You tell it real, brother. Got any more?" But my head was splitting so I left. Petra the acupuncturist thinks it's psychosomatic. Stuck me twenty-one times. I'll wait a few days, see my doctor.

Stevie clicks "Send," logs off, pushes the chair back, decides to make toast. He uses his incomparable, outlandishly priced, Made in Spain, NAFTA approved, Krups fool-proof ("Fuckin doofus proof," as Sgt. Bride would say. Bride, shot so impeccably), deluxe, white toned, smooth shelled, quite nearly noiseless, two-slice toaster. Stevie twists open the plastic bread sack, daintily drops one slice into the left slot, one into the right.

"Yes, sir," he says, saluting the phantom white refrigerator. "It's a wonderful toaster.

IT'S A FUCKING PERFECT TOASTER. IT'S THE MOST BEAUTIFUL FUCKIN TOASTER OF ALL FUCKIN TIME."

Pressing the plastic "Start" bar, Stevie beholds the filament rods heating to brilliant red. Six times, in tight three minute intervals, the caramelized shards spring up. Six times Stevie flinches. It is a good meal. A simple meal. Wolfed down in seconds. Stevie sweeps the crumbs off the kitchen counter with the ridge of his palm, then flicks off the kitchen light. When he lies down to sleep, his dreams are not pleasant.

At dawn he gathers up the crimson blanket which lay heaped on the floor. *Bunch up! Bunch up! Like ghosts! Don't bunch up! Don't!* He makes his bed, hurling sheets forward, folding neat hospital corners, doubling the blanket back four inches over itself, tight-tucking neat square edges all the way round. After dressing, Stevie sits at the computer and boots up. Cindy has written.

Subject: Acupuncture
Date: 30 May 2001 6am
From: Mimsypearl
To: Silverspartan

It might be related to Memorial Day...duh! See your doctor! It's beautiful outside. Have you been out? Beautiful.

Stevie snickers to himself. She certainly is good at that. Rubbing in salt, licking it off. Bitch! May is a cruel month for Stevie. He can tell from his dreams.

Subject: Sleepless and Counting

Date: Tuesday 30 May 2001 6:21am
From: Silverspartan
To: Mimsypearl

It never occurred to me to add one plus one. When you're the center of the storm it's hard to know what coast is where. Go easy, Fraulein. Here's a dream I had.

Stevie hunts down one of many nightmare files, pastes text to body. He marvels how the mind's inner logic has captured his feelings. Would she understand? He trusts Cindy, enjoys her carefree nature, though she does not yet know about the letter sent home or weekly visits to Doctor Foster.

"0900 HOURS. TIME TO MAKE THE DOUGHNUTS," Stevie shouts, heading toward the bathroom.

Toilet, tub, sink. He pinches a sweet white worm onto frayed plastic bristles, shoves the angled stick into his "O" shaped mouth. Pumping the brush forward and back, foam and spittle streaking his chin, Stevie spits, then reads aloud the framed, aging letter, reclaimed after they died, now poised above the medicine cabinet:

"Dear Folks,

Today was a good day. We came up to this hooch and a dink ran out. I emptied a whole magazine into that cocksucker. They don't bleed much, you know. Little fucker had a Smith & Wesson. My lieutenant let me keep it. That's three dinks I've killed so far. Every one I kill I send something home. Last one had a slingshot, remember? Well, be good. Love, Stevie."

Stevie observes himself in the spit-stained mirror. Born mid-century, he has aged well, though his once thick, blonde hair, now gray, receded, he wears neatly trimmed and combed straight back. His eyes, perhaps slightly recessed, hinting at skull, retain their fierce, inscrutable gaze. An ordinary nose, sliced by shrapnel, fits the center of his still youthful face. His cheeks remain angular and smooth, above a strong jaw unjowled by time. Soft pleasant lips perch over a firm, manly chin. Yet despite this appealing countenance, dark clouds swarm across his face, inhabiting his soul.

"Be good...Be good," Stevie mutters, then thrusts his tongue out, rolls his eyes, pivots his head left, right, left, and screams, "MOTHERFUCKAHHH!"

He spits, rinses, backhand wipes his mouth again and again, until the harsh voice grows weak and the reflected image, swollen by tears, abruptly departs.

The monitor has turned pitch black. It is the perfect screen saver. It is the all-time, hands-down, bunker-busting, world's best screen saver. Stevie nudges the machine back to life. After dialing up, he surfs war's history. He pores over colorful maps, imagines helmeted foot soldiers tramping uphill, feels hot kicked wind rushing over his face, hears pounding hooves thudding hard-packed earth, tingles with the absolute delirium of unbridled power wielded by consummate force. It is the perfect way to spend an afternoon. He ducks his head down, wings up one shoulder, wipes sweat from his brow.

"Break time," he trumpets to Spartan emptiness.

Subject: Round 2
Date: 30 May 2001 4pm
From: Mimsypearl
To: Silverspartan

Your dream was vivid, haunting. Did you ever get the Purple Heart? What's an M-79?
I hope you're feeling better.

Stevie reads the letter twice, three times. His emotions choke at the base of his neck. Chess. Now there was a game. A man's game. The salutary compression of flesh and bone redeemed to bantam ranks on rival squares. Duchamp played, as did Beckett. After Hiroshima, Oppenheimer quit. For Stevie, the modern variant, the aptly named five-minute blitz, in street parlance "speed chess," (so well-detailed by K. Ryan in her factual, somewhat over-citationed doctoral thesis, *Outcomes of Antiquity as Applied to Game Theory and Modern Culture*, Michigan State, 1989, (available at http://gametime.ms.edu) truly captivates him, so much so that he has spent considerable time and not immodest sums on obscure theoretic journals, newsletters, closed-cable tournament fees, a thicket of pamphlets, a forest of books. Yes, it is the sight of men (for it is mostly men, and mostly ex-convicts) seated on park benches, hunched over plinth-like tables, the boxy checkered squares dimmed by constant use, the nimble Staunton pieces ever ready to fly, leap, excitedly pounce. It is the mere sight of this static battlefield, this perfect simulacrum, the mobilization of varied pieces for clear and calculable ends, which invigorates Stevie, titillates him, brings him no end of cerebral pleasure. Oh, those Greeks and Persians. How quaint of us. How American of them. Was it not Philidor who said, "Pawns are the soul of chess."

The game begins with lesser pieces amply deployed. Thereafter, keenly circling central squares, each player accelerating the swift one-hand-glide to clock and back, cat-like flanking pawns crawl forward, slow stalking knights advance in cruel L-shaped ambush, rooks appear at sudden King side castles, inscrutable bishops discreetly leer. By mid-game, major pieces spar and slug, rain down sequential hammer blows, unfurl violent exchanges, kick and caterwaul, time stealing past on the spring wound clocks.

"Touch! Touch!" a young, excitable player shouts, snatching a blundered piece, the grand queen helpless, pinned to her King by a stealthy rook. This same player will soon survey his imminent loss.

"One more?" the superior player coyly asks, pocketing money.

Stevie has long admired the experienced men who serenely crush innocent, unsuspecting passers-by, curiosity seekers, the novices or merely maladroit who are their bread and butter. Observing expert players, he thrills at exquisite displays of staggering force, hard-won positions blown full backwards, punched through, without mercy overrun. He revels in shouted staccatos of profane wit, prides himself on seeing four moves deep, spotting clever, well-concealed traps, breathtaking swindles, the well-sprung mate. Yet despite his considerable mastery of gambits, tempo, kings opposition, preferring a Caro-Kann to Alkehine's insidious ploys, endeared as he is to Capablanca's mid-game brilliancies, ever appreciative of Lasker's quixotic end game push-shove-push, Stevie remains deeply puzzled. Most fear to attempt what he most admires: the audacity to risk decisive advance without benefit of logic. For Stevie, this secret fear lays tooled by the fine quill of experience deep in the chambers of his heart. He must write Cindy. A kind letter, Foster would have said. An informative letter.

Subject: Pawn to Queen
Date: 30 May 2001 11:55pm
From: Silverspartan
To: Mimsypearl

Was wondering what you thought about the Sicilian Defense. 1...c5 is the most popular alternative to 1...e5. As soon as White plays d4, Black exchanges the c-Pawn for the d-Pawn. What would you do next? 2. Nc3. 2. Nf3. 2. c3 or 2. d4. Then of course there's the Sheveningen Variation. Or maybe there is no defense.

He will wait for her response. Maybe he could sleep...

At the first high pitched electronic ring, Stevie startles awake. He presses the black plastic phone to his ear.

"Cindy?"

"Good evening, Sir. Are you the breadwinner of the house?"

She is young, naive.

10

"Are you shitting me?"

"I...I beg your pardon?"

"Don't beg. Just get to the goddamn point."

There is a brief, unhealthy silence.

"Sir, if I can have a minute of your time..."

Stevie's words jet from his mouth like thunderous out-going shells, like sleek napalm canisters spinning through air, like the pure pop pop pop of forty mike-mike grenades fired by Cobras going in for the kill.

"This is Silverspartan three-six Indy. The perimeter is secure. My sitreps are negative at this time. How do you copy, over?"

She would say, "I read you Loud and Clear," or "Got you Lucky Chucky." She would say, 'Thank you much. Out."

"Sir. Sir, are you the breadwinner..."

"I SAID MY SITREPS ARE NEGATIVE ARE YOU FUCKIN DEAF?"

Stevie slams the phone down. Hands in his lap, his eye lids fold shut. *I'm praying to you,*

Father. I'm praying. Protect me from invisible forces. Protect me. Father, I'm afraid. Hold me. Give me your strength. Guide me with love. I'm praying to you. Heal me, Father. Heal me. This is how he prays.

For several minutes Stevie sits unnaturally still. He finds the darkness pleasant and lets himself drift to the week before last:

Once seated, he had routinely scanned Foster's soft-lit cubicle. At eye level a dozen gold-stamped diplomas secure the right-side wall, their frames discreetly screwed in place. To the left, pastel museum posters depict flowery gardens, pastoral landscapes, bright-colored boats moored in calm, tranquil water. Scattered across the center, a collection of combat photographs: gaunt-eyed grunts perched in trembling choppers; a sad, weary platoon returned from patrol; an aerial photograph, the grim American fire base desolate, abandoned; a youthful David Foster, full-haired, clean-shaven, thirty pounds lighter, three rows of medals affixed to his chest. Desk. Lamp. Cabinet. The patient's chair is solid and strong.

"How was your week?" said Foster.

Week? Stevie longed to relive his curative past. Yes, the gray fading glory whose dumb stones speak in energetic tongues the anatomy of war. The symmetry of his words, like the hard steely roll of linked tank treads crush all in their path. His voice is pure, caustic, relentless, using third person singular, as if he were someone else:

Second day Ft. Devens, First Sergeant says, "Where you think you're going?" Stevie heading out the barracks door.

"What's it look like, fat boy? Stevie won't pull guard duty. See you in three days."

Stevie returns, they bust him in rank. A cook wakes him. "Get up. You got KP."

Stevie says, "I don't pull KP."

Cook says, "They'll court martial your ass."

Stevie says, "Good. Who gives a fuck? I just want out."

Yes, when Stevie talks to Foster, his words burn like the bright, hissing pendulous swing of magnesium flares, explode like the sharp *BOOMCRACKBOOM* of direct cannon-shell fire, eject like desperate pilots strapped to cold metal chairs who must soon evade enemy capture:

No KP, no haircuts, no saluting. They hated him. Hated him for going up the chain-of-command. "Stevie to see Lieutenant Carter. Stevie to see Major Hitchens, please. Stevie to see Colonel Olecki."

Colonel says, "Why are you making all this trouble, son?"

Stevie says, "Just want out, sir. Out of the Army."

Olecki eye balls Stevie's Cav patch, Combat Medic Badge, other stuff.

"You Cav boys think you're hot shit, don't you?" He tells Stevie, "Straighten up, son, or I will personally court martial your ass." The dumb fuck.

12

Stevie's Army lawyer waits for him but an MP ejects him from JAG.

Stevie says, "You can't do that."

MP says, "Get a fuckin hair cut you piece of shit." Stevie's hair is so long his cunt cap slides off his head.

Stevie hauls ass to the Inspector General. "I'm being court-martialed, sir. I've been denied my right-to-counsel." BOOM!

"I'll look into it," he says. "I'll certainly will look into it."

Stevie is chewed out, restricted to base, put on garbage detail.

A lifer pays him a visit. "Sign here. Bad Conduct Discharge. Isn't that what you want? But Stevie is smart. He has found himself a slick civilian lawyer. "No thanks," he says." Court martial me."

A week later Stevie sees the base head honcho, General Richard R Shultz. His aide-de-camp says, "The general isn't seeing anyone today. GET THE FUCK OUT." He really said that. Get the fuck out!"

At the court martial...

Stevie lowered his head, pinched the space above his irregular nose.

"Six months hard labor, Dishonorable Discharge," Stevie said to Foster.

Stevie had attempted laughter, but fell silent. Silent, like the fatal dead calm between incoming shells, like the shocked-out point man returning from morning patrol, like the thick metal gears of shot-down Cobras scattered in jungle heavy with rain.

"What's most bothering you?" Foster inquired.

And Stevie blurted out the single word "Cambodia."

"What about Cambodia?" Foster said.

"May is Cambodia. Every goddamn year."

He looked inward. Felt salty drops crawl down his face.

BOOM! *They had waited, blown the mines, fired their weapons, advanced when the howling stopped. The perforated dead, not yet transfigured, lay sprawled in waxy tableaux.*

"Lieutenant Gill yells, "Chieu Hoi!" but the dink swings his AK up and the LT wastes him point-blank, the machine-gunner blows his head off. I mean you can look down his fuckin neck, his fuckin spinal column, count the fuckin vertebrae for Christ's sake."

"Then what?"

Stevie paused. His voice went low.

We scavenge the bodies, march, set up an NDP. Lieutenant Gill is holding his jaw like it hurts. "It's nothing, sir. Nothing. You'll be alright."

"Purple Heart," he says. "Doc, you gonna put me in for the Purple Heart?"

Stevie says, "Are you shitting me, Lieutenant? Are you shitting me? It's just skull fragments from the dead dink. You didn't get shot. You didn't get hit. No way I'm putting you in for a medal, sir. No fuckin way."

Foster repeated his question when Stevie failed to respond. "What else?

Two months later Stevie's replacement is dead, half the platoon wasted, but he is safe dragging fifty-five gallon drums from LZ mortar box shitters. He pours diesel, chucks trip flares, stirs the shit soup with a ten foot pole until it's burned down to ash. "What'cha doing, Doc?"

The artillery crews can't believe it. "Burning shit?" Assholes! But Stevie is short. Twenty-three and a wake up.

Then a lifer says, "Get your gear. Charlie Company needs a medic."

Stevie says, "No way. No fuckin way." Until a Major with a grease gun says, "Do it."

Immediately Foster asked the dumbest question of all fuckin time.

"What were you feeling?"

Stevie burst out laughing, then spoke:

"Stevie grabs his weapon, frags, helmet, pack, walks to

14

the chopper pad. The door gunner yells' Hop the fuck in' But Stevie doesn't move.

They sky up. Second bird, Stevie says, "Quan Loi?"

"Yeah. Get on. Get on." Fifteen minutes later he jumps off, walks to battalion. He knows who gave the order.

It happened quickly. From ten meters Stevie pushed the safety switch to Full Automatic. 'ARE YOU SENDING STEVIE OUT? MOTHERFUCKER! ARE YOU SENDING HIM OUT?'

The new medical officer raised both hands over his head. "It was a mistake. I'll send someone else. You don't have to go."

Stevie walked straight past that prick, that PRICK, threw down his gear..."

Foster asked, "Who's Stevie?"

When Stevie stopped sobbing, Foster said, "You're chasing ghosts. You don't need them anymore."

Waiting for the Internet connection, Stevie sifts through old letters Cindy has sent. He scans whole pages, skips entire paragraphs, rifles an entire year of correspondence, settles on Sasha.

Subject: Sasha
Date: 5 December 1998 8:32am
From: Mimsypearl
To: Silverspartan

I had to have Sasha put down last night. yesterday morning I took her to the vet because she wasn't eating. he said she was in kidney failure. did a sonogram that showed a tumor on the urethra. I asked what are her chances if we do surgery. he said, "about zero". I said I wanted to take her home to spend one more night with me. couldn't he sedate her? he said yes, but she'd be sedated and uncomfortable. I asked how come she wasn't crying if she was in pain. he said animals hunker down, find the dark, keep quiet when they're

hurt. otherwise might be hunted down. I looked into her eyes.
she looked at me then looked away. I held her. she weighed
5.8 lbs, down from 7.6 a couple of months ago. I wanted to
scream. I asked him if he was staying late just for this. he
shrugged his shoulders. I signed the papers. he gave her
something to make her go slowly asleep and left me alone
with her. I could feel her weight sag. I didn't know what to
do. I just stood there holding her. finally he came back in and
gave her the injection. the nurse had to come in. I asked why.
he said to hold her. but she wasn't moving. the nurse asked
me if I was ok. I said "no." then they left me alone with her
again. she was heavy. her head bobbed. I didn't know what to
do. finally they came back. I said I wanted to take the body
and bring it back the next day so they could cremate her. they
said it was hot. not a good idea. but ok if I wanted to. I went
back in and looked at her eyes. she wasn't there. so I walked
out and said never mind–I don't want the body. they said will
you be alright driving home by yourself. I said I don't know.
I stopped to buy gas on the way home. the attendant came out
because I couldn't figure out where to put the credit card,
how to put the nozzle in. the guy got annoyed, did everything
for me. I said I had just had my cat put to sleep. he said the
gas prices were actually higher than shown and started to
change the signs. I'm sitting here in my apt and sasha is
everywhere. and nowhere.

It was a good letter. A wonderful letter. Sincere and
heartfelt. Stevie loved her. Even if she couldn't understand
what drove him, uncoiled him, what each day drove
transformed men to shoot and shoot, or shake with fear, or
cry out from perfidious, improvident wounds, or seek
revenge, yes, grow accustomed to it, yes, love it, yes, the
blood-lust killing, search and find them, yes, hunt them down
like dogs, they are hunting too, yes, do you understand,
Cindy, they are hunting and we are hunting. Oh Cindy, yes,
yes, was it not ever so: we hunted and killed each other in
order to survive. My dearest, dearest sweet and lovely Cindy

was it not Pindar's fate to render in hard set stone, "Oh passerby, go tell the Spartan's we lie here in obedience to their laws."

Sweet, dulcet, simple Cindy. She had lost her cat. Her dumb-fuck shit-ass cat. Heat rushed to Stevie's face. Rockets, mortars, ambush, monsoon. We lived and loved and killed like dogs. Don't you get it? Oh, Christ. Oh, Cindy. Oh, passerby. Yes, we lay down like obedient dogs. Yes, my darling Cindy who dares to listen, who does not turn away, who remains ever faithful, Cindy of the ever fuckin-stupid questions, yes, so ever stupid I want to choke you, choke you, yes, yes, I want to slit your throat, just once, straight across, see fresh blood spurt in spiraled beats across your well-kept home. Oh loving, lovely Cindy, who cares for Stevie, accepts him, does not turn her back, or shy away, or make unkind remarks: what do you know about death? What? And what do you know about war? Stevie flinched. No. NO. He pummeled and struck ever widening circles in callous, empty air. It was not possible. He would not allow it. Foster could not be right. Overwhelmed, Stevie lay down beneath the red blanket, sunk his face into a yielding white cloud and curled himself to sleep. In the dream, he made love to her. Long, full, luxuriant love. Afterwards, he drew himself over her, dotted sweet kisses across her luminous mouth. "I'm kissing you, Cindy," his dream self said.

He woke as usual, as if suddenly tugged. The cooling fan whirred inside the computer. Its black plastic fins recalled spent mortar shells poking out from dry blasted earth. Delayed fuse, direct impact, dread aerial burst, each had its fearful effect. Men were crudely blown in half, or neatly cleaved by fiery shards, or blasted backwards, or up, or died intact, or lived, though naked, or simply bled to death in static end game stature. It was a good weapon. A cruel weapon. *He had left the computer on all night.*

"Fourth time this week," said Stevie, seating himself at his desk.

17

He waited for the dark faceless square to chameleon bloom; waited as the modem snapped invisible things to perfect place, then clicked the appropriate button.

Subject: Weaponry
Date: 30 May 2001 7:12am
From: Silverspartan
To: Mimsypearl

An M-79 was a very large bore, single shot rifle which resembled a blunderbuss. It fired fist sized 40mm shells in three flavors: buckshot, high explosive, and magnesium flares. In the jungle it was a good weapon. The North Vietnamese Army favored it over the M-16, which tended to jam and was hard to fix. Their standard weapon was much better. They were excellent soldiers too. I was lucky. Never wounded. My lieutenant once shot a VC at close range. He caught a few dents. Nothing serious. Asked me to put him in for the Purple Heart. I said no. Well, time to make the donuts.

Her reply was instantaneous.

Subject: Purple Haze
Date: 31 May 2001 7:21am
From: Mimsypearl
To: Silverspartan

What's with the numeric code? I didn't know you were in Sicily. Sounds like the M-79 was the best one, if you couldn't get the AK-47. See, I did my homework. Questions: Why didn't you want to recommend him for the purple heart? "Had shot a VC at close range." But in self-defense, no? Are you free tomorrow night?

Stevie drummed the keyboard. "X X X X." Cross bones. Only the skull was missing. He pondered the startling sight of a brainless head which he once peered into. The soft iridescent lining suggested a fish pulled from water. Only the fish was a man and the man did not move and in strange repose seemed at rest.

Stevie lowered his head. Morning sunlight danced small circles across the bare white walls. Outside, cicadas trilled their high-pitched tune. The effect was hypnotic. The fall into green time was sudden and brief.

("She's a fuckin dink," the machine gunner said, wiping blood from his boots. When Stevie knelt down the gunner rushed forward. The lieutenant pushed him aside. "No. We got enough today. She's POW. Go ahead, Doc." And Stevie pressed his canteen to enemy lips, suckling her back to life.)

Code. Numeric code. Beginning. Middle. End game. It was quiet now. Stevie looked about. He gathered his thoughts. Sacrifice. He must do that.

Subject: Lieutenant's Purple Heart Club Banned
Date: 31 May 2001 7:49am
From: Silverspartan
To: Mimsypearl

Hey Cindy,

Bet you're off to work. Story for another day that Purple Heart. Please understand.

Stevie stood up and walked to the kitchen. He began cursing. Louder, then louder still, unmercifully hurling abuse with each strident step. He would kick and kick the great white boxy beast. He would shatter all windows with his battering hands. He would crack brick walls by the force of his skull. He would scream and shout and blister with rage. Purple Heart? You want the Purple Heart? What about Corson? Shot through the lungs. And Bride. Six days and a wake up. What about the poor bastard you replaced? Sniped once in the hand, once in the head. I tried... I tried. Jesus fuckin Christ, sir. How many times do you need to hear it?

You did not get shot. You did not get hit. Stevie patched you up because you were good. You were very fuckin good.

Nice shooting, sir. But you did not get shot. Not then. Not ever. And therefore, Lieutenant, Stevie still loves you, he will always love you, he will always love all his men, but he no longer gives a flying fuck. Do you read me, sir? Do we have solid copy? All Stevie did was stay alive. That's all he did. Therefore, Lieutenant, Stevie hereby refuses not to have a fuckin future. Or at least he'll fuckin try. With all due fuckin respect, sir, Stevie has got the right to kick the shit out of anybody or anything that keeps him from enjoying the sun, the trees, the snow, the sea, I mean, kick the motherfucker in the balls wants Stevie not to delight in birds or the touch of a woman.

Do you copy? I said do you fuckin copy? Who the fuck are you to get in the way of Stevie's life? You, sir, are but a deciduous memory much in need of sacerdotal dispensation. A ripe bead of shit in the rank outhouse of time. You cannot fucking sweat. You cannot fuckin laugh. Stevie's right to enjoy his life outranks you, Lieutenant, no matter how much he fuckin loves you. No matter what you did for Stevie, he hereby declares, according to Robert's Rules, or the Geneva convention, or the Rig fuckin Veda, or the Mahafuckinbharata, Upanishads, Koran, the Holy fuckin' Bible, the Lotus sutra, the Diamond sutra, the Rajna horse sacrifice, the Hymn of creation, Vishnu, Shiva, master's Basho, Chuan Tzu, Lao Tzu, the fuckin ardent Svetaketu, or He who in heaven is its highest fuckin surveyor. Oh with righteous saintly song and cloistered fuckin choir, my dear, dear, Lieutenant, kindly shove that cursed star deep into the crimson folds of your royal fuckin ass. Yes, yes, Stevie will try hard, hard, to earn new ones. God will bestow them and Stevie will outrank everyone else. Do you copy, sir? Stevie says do you fuckin copy? Good. That's real good. Cause Stevie's going AWOL from his memory's stockade and the enemy? The enemy is you, sir. And Stevie will give it his best shot, the motherfuckin best shot of all fuckin time, and you, sir, you will be wasted.

The words resounded a hundred times in the center of his soul.

When Stevie returned to his room he spoke to the empty monitor as if to a mentor, redeemer, best lover, friend.

"Damn you, Lieutenant," he said. "You son-of-a-bitch."

Then, with eyes half shut Stevie smiled a vague prelapsarian press-lipped grin. The kind which appear on smooth stone-faced bodhisattvas lost in gold leaf bliss. The kind which grace those who by supreme martial will, stupendous luck or, paradoxically, dark Jobean nights, heart sundering Jesuitic loss, arrive when sorrow and doubt–twin pillars of pilgrims misery–are sacrificed, surrendered, in a word-cast out. In the photography of his mind Stevie, who stood at convincing parade rest, recollected the event which had long steeped him in secret sorrow:

The casualty lay huddled inside the burning bunker. "C'mon," Stevie shouted, eyeing the stacked wood boxes packed with dull green hand grenades. "C'mon. This thing's gonna blow." But the wounded man could not hear him. Without thought Stevie crawled into the smoky pit and dragged him out. Months later someone said, "They got something for you, Doc. Better clean yourself up."

In fresh fatigues and shined boots Stevie had walked toward the company formation. Lieutenant Gill pointed him to place. Stevie looked expectantly at each man. In the relentless heat they stared straight back. A color guard, bright banners sagging, approached in strict, angular step. The lieutenant maintained silence. A major took hold of Stevie's fatigue shirt; a colonel read the citation. And they gave him the Silver Star.

"Fuck the computer," said Stevie, settling with pad and pencil on the bedroom floor. He missed the frictive feel of sharpened lead to white bleached paper. Taking his time, Stevie adjusted the triangulated pressure of thumb, middle and index finger around the easily snapped yellow implement.

It began simple enough, the polite use of discursive

language, comfortable in length, moderate in detail, deft in plying crack bon mot's and high-spirited phrases, the occasional four-letter word, the patois of war. Then came hurried diagrams depicting land and no-man's-land, the dread L-shaped ambush, the trip-wire detonated automatic ambush (composed of illegal Claymore mines staked at ground level, each sleek curved box contained two kilograms of C-4 plastic explosive and many hundred steel bearings), the slow accordion-rippling push of wide eyed men stagger-stepping forward on daily patrol. At length, he wrote heart-felt cameos of the men in his platoon, brief Aurelian meditations, cordial *pensees*. He did not mean to pour himself out on the page, attempting instead through varied and calibrated circumstance to convey the qualities of combat and what remained afterward. Stevie tried hard not to scold Cindy, nor berate, or patronize or impart canard, but state in practical detail the unerring chaos, the unpredictable beat, the cyclic consequences, the sorrow of war.

Of course Stevie wept. He heard and saw again the grand slam bang of corsairing artillery shells, the startling, high rising screams, the grotesque onion layers of organ and bone. He felt the lively kick and caterwaul above descending parachute flares; the *WRAP-WRAP-WRAP* of helicopters racing to attack. And always, always, the single word men used when calling for help: "Medic!" And Stevie would bind them and heal them, reveal impossible truths, provide comfort and care for those that lived. And, thus deceived, they took him and trusted him as one of their own. All this he wrote down, knowing full well Cindy could not know what she had not witnessed first-hand, and therefore, yes, Stevie would forgive her, just as he himself would never, ever forget.

Subject: Tickets
Date: 1 June 2001 7:23 am
From: Mimsypearl

To: Silverspartan

A friend gave me two tickets to "Miss Saigon." Are you free tomorrow night?

Stevie stared at the screen, then replied:

Subject: Just the Ticket
Date: 1 June 2001 7:30 am
From: Silverspartan
To: Mimsypearl

"Miss Saigon? Sounds like fun."

Off The Road

In 1995, having backpacked through Singapore, Thailand, and Laos, I flew from Vientiane to Hanoi, traveled down the coast, and caught a motorcycle to Saigon's Long Distance Bus Station. It was not a planned pilgrimage, though events would turn out in that direction. The ride to An Loc cost sixty cents and took ninety minutes. There were no foreigners, only Vietnamese. Where would I stay? Who and what would I meet? And what of Quan Loi? These were magnetic questions to me.

When the bus lurched to a grinding halt in An Loc's neatly tiled center I grabbed my gear and jumped off. Immediately a crowd gathered about me—a thin, weary tourist. A gaunt, soft-spoken man who later became my guide led me to the tumbledown Binh Long Hotel.

"Here OK," said Thanh. "Other place expensive."

Cramped and stuffy, my two dollar a night room had a single hard mattress, torn mosquito netting, and a solitary wood hatched window. At night the heat was unbearable. Mornings, the Binh Long's communal bathroom was packed with noisy transient Asian men. The Chinese style squat latrines were not pleasant.

The following day Thanh and I rode his battered Honda Cub to Quan Loi. I knew I would find American sand bag bunkers, artillery cannons, culvert hooches, the rubber trees merciful shade. After a breezy twenty minutes, Thanh pulled over and parked the scooter.

"Why are we stopping?" I asked. My heart dropped when Thanh said, "This is Quan Loi."

In fact, the huge American base is gone now, flat as a field, the once smooth tarmac airstrip crumpled and washed away. The rest of Quan Loi was covered by bush and scrub and its signature red dirt.

The heat was unbearable. I poked around, plucked an AK47 cartridge, rusted and brittle, from the sun baked soil. I took photographs: The remains of the strip, the land where the base once stood; a group of peasants planting corn. The ghosts of their dead filled their faces.

A sad, weather-beaten man wearing a tattered American army shirt who spoke English said he was fifty-five years old; he appeared seventy. He said during the war he had worked with the First Cavalry Division. I asked him if he could locate LZ Compton.

"Yes," he replied, pointing north, then pulled out his pockets, which were empty and flat, like elephant ears. "With Americans I had money and food. I had house. Now I am nothing."

I turned aside so he would not see my face, then pressed fifty thousand dong, two weeks salary, into his hand. A few minutes later I asked a colorfully dressed woman where she lived. After Than translated she raised her thin weary arm, pointed due east, and spoke a few words in the beautiful sing song lilt of her language. Thanh said the village was two miles away. I looked about. All the peasants, young and old, wore sandals ground down beyond repair.

As we walked the area Thanh said at war's end scavengers and resettled peasants stripped the base clean. Sought after scrap metal was carted away; artillery cannons were stolen; homes were built from American timber. For years unexploded ordnance posed a constant danger; only recently has it been cleaned up. Still, he said, beneath the soil Vietnam is littered with buried mortar and artillery shells, rotting 40 mm grenades, high explosive five-hundred pound bombs. Much land is permeated with Agent Orange. To this day all take their toll on the Vietnamese people.

As the noon sun continued to beat straight down Thanh suggested we visit Lake Xosim.

"I think you will like," he said.

I said goodbye to the peasants, to Quan Loi, and hopped on the back of his scooter.

The Cub raced forward over the American blacktop. In minutes the hot rushing air dried our sweaty clothes.

The sleepy village surrounding the lake seemed untouched by time. Small neat houses with terracotta roofs encircled the clear and tranquil waters. Low brambled coffee plants edged the lake perimeter. Exquisite open-air pagodas with graceful walkways served as landing docks. I watched a fisherman grip and sway and cast his expanding net.

Two hundred meters out, at the lake's center, a skeletal bamboo platform stood eerily silent. "No one swim here now," he said, and pantomimed drinking whiskey." After holiday, too many people drown." According to custom their spirits haunted the water.

"I want to show you something else," he said.

We walked a short ways through partially cleared jungle. The remains of an old French fort, built completely of stone, rose up heavy and hypnotic. The laughter of children playing badminton echoed off the moss-covered stones. Thanh looked at me, but I could not speak.

That evening I met Ba, manager at the Binh Long hotel. Short, trim, and pleasant, like Thanh, he too had worked for the Americans. After the war, Ba said the NVA had rounded them up, sent him and Than to re-education camps. When asked what that meant he would not tell me.

"What is the English for big machines that push earth?" he asked instead.

I closed my eyes a moment. "Bulldozers?"

Ba nodded grimly. "We put bodies in big holes after

fighting."

In a soft voice he described the ferocious battle that took place in An Loc in 1972. I listened intently. I'd never heard of it before. Ba said thousands of North Vietnamese troops, tanks and artillery, fought a pitched battle against the American backed ARVN (Army of the Republic of Vietnam). He said American B 52 strikes and attack helicopters pounded the NVA, killed them like animals, but they just kept coming. Than said after seven months of chaos and carnage tens of thousands on both sides had been killed or maimed, the town literally pulverized.

"An Loc still wounded," he said. "Blood everywhere. Blood you cannot see."

Late at night on the third day I had unexpected visitors.

"Wake up! Wake up!" said Ba, repeatedly pounding on the wood door. "The police are here. They wish to speak with you.

"I'm sleeping," I said. "Tell them 'go away.' Tell them I'll talk tomorrow."

In my travels I'd learned not to be pushed around by authorities. Still, what could they want? On the first day, I handed a copy of my passport (never once giving the real item at any guest house) to the hotel clerk. But few foreigners visited An Loc, and she had put it aside. Informed of my presence the police tracked me down.

"You come out. You please talk with them," Ba demanded.

Given the urgent tone in his voice, I quickly dressed and unlocked the door. In the narrow hallway, two thin officers, identical in green caps and green uniforms, pressed a litany of questions.

"Where is your passport? How long you stay? Have you drugs? Have you camera? Where are you travel to An Loc?"

Vietnam remains a secretive culture. Ba, standing erect, dutifully translated. It was clear that not cooperating would cause trouble. I agreed to visit police headquarters.

"In the morning," I said.

The police accepted my offer. As they turned to go Ba nodded, secretly pleased.

In the dawns sweet cool air Thanh and I drove past thick, impenetrable jungle, past infinite rows of stately rubber trees, at last arriving at a squat one-story building on the town's outskirts. Inside a damp, musty, ill-lit room, several American carbines hugged a mildewed wall. Their battered wood stocks once embracing gleaming gun metal, were dull and pitted. A policeman pointed to a school child's chair. For nearly an hour I filled out tissue-thin forms in triplicate.

That afternoon, riding a borrowed bike I returned to the haunting rows of symmetrical rubber, strung my GI hammock between two slender trees and slept while mosquitoes hummed and bit. Waking at dusk, covered with itching welts, I rode back to town and chatted with Thanh's family.

Toward 9 p.m. his wife and young daughter decided to go to sleep. As a light rain tapped on the roof, Thanh spoke lovingly of his daughter, her plans for the future. "She wishes to attend university," he said, "study to be doctor."

The hours passed quickly. When it was time to go I embraced him. In a very short time we had become close. How it happened I did not understand.

The following day I stumbled upon the town hospital. Ba had said that during the battle the ARVN used it as fighting position. He'd said the NVA, holed up in the Police Station, shelled the hospital with rockets and heavy artillery. Walking the abandoned hospital grounds, I stared in awe at split-open buildings, the walls pocked by bullets and skittering shrapnel. I drew diagrams on notebook paper, inspected dark and dank surgical wards. There were no medical supplies. Just rooms. Dozens of empty rooms.

In one nearly intact building I met a middle-aged female doctor who spoke excellent English. Somewhat evasively she said, "I try my best to treat my patients. But sometimes there is nothing to do." She glanced at a pale unconscious young woman who lay on an rusting American gurney.

"Attempted suicide," she said. "Poison"

At night, I heard enormous trucks rumble through town from ten till dawn. Ba said these were timber convoys hauling illegal wood from Cambodia. Each trailer lugged fifty immense logs held fast by heavy link chains. Hurried red numbers were chalked over the stiff raw trunks; they could have been bodies.

Four days later I stood outside the Binh Long Hotel, waiting to leave An Loc. When the bus arrived, Thanh and I embraced one last time. Much was said in those final moments. I've written him since and received replies, though money sent went missing.

"First Loc Ninh then Bo Dop," I said, waving farewell.

It grew dark. A light rain began to fall. But as the bus pulled out I knew I could face what lay ahead.

The bus to Loc Ninh cost thirty-cents and took twenty-five minutes. Just the sound of the name brought back memories.

In dense jungle, except for the bullet holed fuselage the Cobra gun ship is nearly intact. Its long slender rotor blades reach upward to the sun. No one speaks as we file past the wounded thing, its large shiny gears throbbing in tropical dirt. No signs of struggle. No drag marks. No one looks back.

Past the grim town center I took a room in a shabby concrete block hotel. An hour later I flagged down a man with a motorcycle. Trong spoke good English. "OK," he said accepting the offer to be my guide.

"Most time only MIA teams come to Loc Ninh," he said.

"Why is that?" I asked.

Trong parked his bike under a shade tree. With his right hand he traced the plummeting arc of American choppers. "In 1972 everyone fight here. ARVN, NVA, special Americans. Many people die. No one win."

A friendly woman, a long ugly scar ran the length of her

brow, the manager of the cement hotel joined us.

"Me hit by rocket," she said, smiling as she pressed her fingers to the cruel gash in her skull. "My daughter five year. My daughter dead." A dreadful grin filled her child-like face.

"Problem," said Trong, pointing to approaching headlights.

Minutes later the police ordered me out of Loc Ninh.

"Show me your papers. Why are you here? What do you want?" the officer yelled.

Through Trong I yelled back at him, "I fought here. I want to look around. I want to find the American firebase. I know it's here. I know it."

What was it about this thin gaunt man that angered me, made me feel we'd met before? Was it his thick straight black hair? His high prominent cheek bones? His rigid posture and sinewy build?

We continued to shout until Trong said, "He NVA colonel. You show respect."

"What do you know about war?" the colonel snarled.

The game was Poker. We played by candle light, using bullets for money. When the first mortars hit everyone scattered. The exploding shells shook the earth then crept south, pounding the far side of the base. When it ended I crawled out of the bunker. The card table was blown to pieces. Medics carried the wounded on stretchers. The dead were arranged in stately rows. Someone's brains lie in a puddle of blood.

"Get out," said the colonel, livid. "You must leave An Loc."

His rage only excited me. "I'm cold and tired. It's late. I have a room. I haven't eaten. I need sleep," I said.

The colonel stared at Trong in disbelief. Trong looked away.

"All right," I said, "I'll leave tomorrow."

"Then give me your passport," the colonel scowled. "And go back to your room and stay inside."

"No," I said. It felt good to fight back, maybe find whatever it was he wanted kept hidden. "I'll give you a copy." I unbuttoned my shirt, opened my money belt, plucked out a paper square and handed it to him. "Here," I snapped. "Keep it."

The officer glared at me, but I turned my back on him and walked away, satisfied that I had stood my ground. Months later I would learn how lucky I was not to have been arrested. Or worse. Trong was right. I should have shown respect.

After dinner I lay down, tossed and turned in my cavernous room, rose early, and caught the first bus out.

"Here, I want to go here," I would tell drivers, pedestrians, street vendors, anyone who would listen as I pointed to the red square inch of Song Be province on a glossy fifty-cent map bought in Saigon. "I'm trying to find LZ Compton."

Why didn't they know about its perimeter ringed with sandbagged bunkers, its steel drum showers, mess tent with hot meals, its no-mans-land studded with barbed wire and booby traps? Didn't they know about its Howitzer cannons and mortar crews, the reinforced aid station packed with medical supplies? Didn't they care after weeks of we walk into them into us or we walk into each other, or they ambush us, or we ambush them, Compton, even with its oozing monsoon mud, its limitless dry season dust and heated squalor, its constant threat of rocket or mortar or ground attack, didn't these slender, black haired, wheat skinned, darting eyes, industrious Asian people know that after weeks in the jungle Compton meant bunkers and guard duty and good food and that was a good thing, a very good thing? Didn't they know that? Didn't they? How could they not know or care about these things?

It would be there. Just as we'd left it. Compton. Just the sound of the name brought back memories.

"Here. I want to go here," I would say, jabbing the map again and again.

After the third time in two days heading to the wrong town on National Highway 13, I hollered, "Stop!" The peasants on the sweltering bus giggled when I jumped off in the middle of nowhere but I was livid and lost and nothing mattered. I just didn't care anymore.

Jungle edging both sides of the road, I threw down my pack, sat on it, and wept. A minute later a crowd of well-mannered children gathered round.

"Where-are-you-from?   What-is-your-name? How-old-you-are?" they sweetly badgered. I sat silent as stone until they too gave up and departed.

All save for a dear child who pedaled her blue bike in tight, uniform circles, and in perfect English asked, "What do you want, sir? My father can help you. Please, sir. Where do you want to go?"

As if she were the adult I lamented, "Go away. I don't need anything. Just go away."

I hitched, got lost, snared a ride at a checkpoint from a fat, slick-haired cop.

"You wait," he said, then returned, gripping the handlebars of a 1500cc Kawasaki. I hopped on and threw my arms around his ample waist, (careful to avoid the holstered U.S. Army .38 caliber pistol) as we sped fifty miles an hour to the same wrong town.

"This Song Be," he said, his right fist sweeping the air. A welcoming billboard read, "Tu Dao Mot." I smiled. He zoomed off, a puff of blue smoke trailing behind the engine's loud roar. The search for LZ Compton had ended.

I hoisted my pack and trudged to a nearby restaurant. Once seated, the cheerful waitress, a former American employee, introduced her supervisor, an elder woman with a slender build.

"She NVA. In war, she shoot me," said the waitress.

The supervisor cocked her hand, pistol-like, and put it to her subordinate's head.

"Now we friend," the waitress tittered.

The happy pair watched me pluck stale noodles from a chipped ceramic bowl. The thin gruel was tasteless. A full plate of fruit salad was superb.

Refreshed, I walked down a wide black road dotted with flimsy shops and spindly trees that stood scourged and withered. Dark heavy clouds loomed overhead. I spotted a corrugated metal porch roof a hundred meters away. The sky turned coal black, streaks of lightning snapped across the horizon. I walked as fast as I could. It began to rain. None too soon, I huddled beneath the tin roof; a moment later the wooden door creaked open. Nguyen, short and wiry, invited me inside his neat, cozy house. He introduced me to his wife, a shy thin woman who smiled diminutively. He flicked on the light of a large aquarium. A large goldfish swam indifferently back and forth. Nguyen reached into a bookcase, selected a volume, and proudly opened his 1985 BMW repair manual.

"Before American's I work in Germany," he said, holding the book like a bible. Outside, sheets of rain swept over the roof; torrents swamped the street. Closing the book, Nguyen said, "Soon, we look for hotel."

When the rain stopped Nguyen disappeared into a small room, then wheeled out a shiny Honda Cub. His wife opened the front door.

"Good meeting," she said. We touched palms. On the porch, Nguyen mounted the bike, inserted a key, and began the ritual of kick starting. On the fourth try a throaty roar and lush black plume announced success.

I hopped on behind him. Off we sped, the wheels cutting a path through flooded alleys and nameless streets, until we suddenly arrived at a bland, dismal building which appeared empty. My hopes skyrocketed. Nguyen switched off the motor. "I wait," he said.

Inside, a young gaunt-faced clerk wearing wire-rim spectacles said, "Passport..." Reluctantly, I handed the prized document to him. His gaze fastened on the gold stamped American eagle, one talon clutching an olive branch, the other a cluster of thirteen arrows. He looked at me full in the face, wagged a finger in the air.

"No foreigner allowed," he said, then muttered, "Sorry."

I felt sad but excited by the uncertainty of not knowing what lay ahead.

Nguyen patted the back of his seat. "I show you more."

We drove to a monolithic five-story building whose drab cement blocks alternated with large rectangular windows. A hundred canvas curtains blocked out Vietnam's delicate setting sun. I pushed open the large glass doors, walked into the spacious foyer. A pleasant young woman with long black hair sat behind a large wood desk.

She looked at me as if I was a dead thing. "Forty dollar one night," she said.

I was a backpacker, not a businessman. A soldier, not a civilian. What's wrong with these people? What's wrong with them?

I walked out. It would be dark soon. Where would I eat? Where would I sleep? Undaunted, Nguyen made for Thu Dau Mot's Central Station.

"You go Saigon," he yelled, as the hot wind flattened our hair and pelted our faces.

Slowed by evening traffic we entered the depot as the last crowded bus rolled off into the night.

"Take taxi!" Nguyen hollered above the urban din.

I hopped off the Cub. "Here," I said, and flourished money.

"No!"

Cars honked, impatient cyclists gunned their engines. We shook hands. Nguyen vanished. Inside a grimy American station wagon, twelve skinny passengers vied for impossible comfort. A lovely Chinese woman squished tight against me explained the riddle of Song Be. "People no understand map. Name change many time in war. Also, some people crazy."

Sweaty and swayed by the sleepless road, we drifted past small, impoverished towns, emerald rice paddies, exhausted peasants hunkering down for the night. Several times I shook myself awake. Weeks, or was it years ago, a Vietnamese monk had warned me, "Always watch your things. The people steal." I dropped my guard and slept.

Waking at Saigon's Long Distance Bus Station I checked my gear, crawled out, and headed for the main road. An alert cyclo driver pulled up, and tried to hustle me.

"Where you go? I take. Two dollah. Two dollah. Where you go?"

I shook my head. "Too much," I muttered, shouldered my pack and walked away.

"One dollah..."

"No."

"How much? How much?" he pleaded.

I looked at the haggard man and recalled what Thanh had finally said one night at An Loc as we sat with Ba. At wars end the NVA had rounded up all ARVN and American sympathizers, he said. The "re-education camps" were stark prisons where beatings and starvation were common.

"Like this," Ba said, suddenly lifting his shirt, revealing his scars.

Than said ARVN officers who survived the ordeal often found work driving cyclos.

"Fifty cents," I said. My voice was cold, uncaring. I had never worked with ARVN but they were known to run from battle. The pack grew heavy. I began walking away. He knew I was bluffing but that's the way it worked.

"OK...OK. Get in."

The haggard man gave a sigh then pushed down hard on the bicycle pedal. The pedicab lurched forward, slowly picking up speed.

The next day I flew to Phnom Penh. At the Capitol Guest House a stifling cinder block room with bed and sink cost three dollars a night. Every morning on the adjacent street a dozen young Cambodian men with motorbikes vied to whisk backpackers wherever they wished to go.   "Take me...take me..." they shouted and waved as tourists drew near.

For some reason, I chose Elephant Man. Burly and gruff, with a full moon-like face, he told me the Khmer Rouge had killed most of his family, he was lucky to live.

"Pol Pot no good," he said as we pulled up to the entrance of a large flat field.

A sleepy teenaged boy, wearing shorts and flip flops, motioned us in. Elephant Man parked his bike and led the way.

"Look close," he said, pointing to several grassy pits.

Everywhere I looked scraps of cloth flecked the earth. It wasn't possible, was it? The boy lay down beneath the shadow of a tall wooden tower filled top to bottom with neatly arranged rows of skulls and bones. In the war I had seen my share of fresh or putrid bodies, or sun-bleached bones poking up out of shallow graves. I had watched and helped desecrate the dead. And consecrate ours. But not like this. Or was the boy inured or overwhelmed by it all, or simply tired from the noon day heat?

Elephant Man pointed to the horizon, his hand sweeping left to right. "More," he said, in a cold flat voice, as if the life had been squeezed from it. "Much more."

I bought two Cokes from a rusting American soda machine. Both of us were sweated up and guzzled the icy drinks down.

After a time Elephant Man asked, "Where next?" but for several minutes I could not speak.

"Capitol Hotel," I finally said. "Tomorrow, Ministry of Information."

"Why you want?" he asked, as I hopped on the bike.

But I would not tell him. Back at the hotel I ate a simple meal then fitfully slept for the next twelve hours.

His threadbare clothes hung limp against his body. We both knew I was lying.

"Here," said the clerk at the Ministry of Information.

In the coolness of the one-story wood building I filled out

the mimeographed form, gave him a one inch passport photo, presented a counterfeit resume, pressed an American five-dollar bill to his palm.

"You come back one o'clock," he said, as if nothing had transpired

With the sun high overhead and the temperature rising, I decided to explore the narrow side streets which offered a bit more shade. Wandering about, I poked my head into small crowded shops tucked into stucco buildings weathered delicate shades of pink or blue. I smiled and waved hello to school children dressed in white uniforms, their teacher carefully chalking Khmer script on ancient blackboards. At a French built post office I bought aerograms and admired what remained of a once magnificent chandelier. I checked my watch and headed back to the Ministry of Information.

"For you" said the clerk, handing me a Media Pass encased in stiff transparent plastic. Beneath the words Kingdom of Cambodia, the country's motto: Nation, Religion, King. I nodded a silent thank you to this inscrutable man. His wide mouth formed a diminutive smile. A survivor's smile. Then he was gone.

Three days later I used the pass to obtain an extra week exploring the famous ruins of Angkor Wat. At a guesthouse in the nearby town of Siem Reap, I met Carl, a brooding ex pat American who lived in Kyoto.

"My brother was in Vietnam," he said, one night. "That's why they wouldn't take me. I wanted to go. I wanted to fight."

Carl didn't seem to care what I had to say, which angered me, then made me sad.

At the Merry Guest House I met a shy Japanese girl on the rebound from a broken heart. "My boyfriend leave me," she said, still crying inside.

We spent a day at the spectacular ruins of Ta'Prom, shared a harrowing motorcycle ride through a sudden downpour. Back at the guest house, the two of us drenched, she hugged me tight.

"This best time I have," she said.

"Me too," I whispered.

I flew to the lovely port town of Sihanoukville, took a room at a backpackers hotel. Rob, a heavy-set Boston cabbie in the room next door, smoked hashish and partied with prostitutes.

"Great hash!" he said one morning, exhaling a white plume of smoke.

Through Rob I met Alex, a cheerful Englishman, married to a local woman. Alex said she had escaped the fields of the Khmer Rouge by running for days, hid in the jungle, eluded search patrols, bursts of machine gun fire, lost her infant to a land mine.

"That was twenty years ago," he said, "but she still has nightmares. And kicks in her sleep. Or flies into rages." He shook his head mournfully. "What is it that bothers her? I just don't understand."

Alex sat transfixed while I told him what I knew about PTSD.

"So that's it!" he said, as if the sun had finally broken through a stubborn dark cloud. "So that's it!"

I met Wilhelm, a tall thin Frenchman who'd done two years in Cambodia as a UN Peacekeeper. He spoke Khmer fluently, knew the customs and culture, and a bit more.

One afternoon Wilhelm grabbed my arm and yanked me back from a jungle path.

"It is not safe," he said, politely wagging his finger.

"But..."

We had talked about Vietnam. The trembling fear, the rush of combat, the heady wish to relive danger.

"No," he said. "Just no."

The following week I took a six-hour taxi to Kampong Cham; found a guide; crossed a river by ferry; spent a sweltering day in the hushed haunted ranks of a rubber tree plantation. On the road back to Phnom Penh I saw the terrifying red signs whose skull and bones stood guard over a single word: MINES! So that's what Wilhelm had meant.

I continued traveling in Asia, Indonesia, Europe, then at last flew home. Many years passed before I understood that I had buried the war to avoid my feelings of love and sorrow and loss. It took years to understand that Vietnam was more than a memory of firefights, ambushes, the joy of living one more day, the dread of the next time we walked into them, they walked into us. Though nothing could recapture my youth or the unrepeatable friendships made in combat, it took years to understand that the VC and NVA, the Vietnamese civilians, were human beings no different than us. That was the heart of it. The sorrows and losses both sides felt, the hope to make it meaningful. And maybe, just maybe, one day let it all go.

Torque At Angkor Wat

I am fortunate. I have no have problems with highly charged emotional states. No past events which I cannot discuss. I am lucky. I do not struggle with feelings of loss, feelings of guilt, anger, flashbacks, nightmares. I sleep well. I do not toss or kick or leg cramp or leap at ghosts. I am fortunate. I have not one splinter of conflict within me.

There are two of us in the great tan field of withered grass. It is the heat and drought that have done it. Everywhere the sun disk kills with its merciful light. Only the surrounding jungle, which lords over buried ruins, the leafy sheltering jungle which may harbor unsavory men, only the effervescent green canopy provides shade, here at Preah Khan.

I am wearing faded blue jeans, a white T-shirt and hiking boots. I am thin. It is easy to lose weight backpacking and I have lost thirty pounds in four months. At forty-six I am lithe and muscular. My thick hair is jet black. I'm told I look young for my age. I'm told there are no lines on my face because I do not smile. Often I say to myself "What do they know?" and I say it without malice.

In Cambodia marijuana is sold in open air markets at five dollars per kilo. It is not uncommon to see young tourists huff on long, thick joints. I do not smoke, or drink or take drugs but Jack does.

Jack is an engine of madness. He envies me. Jack wanted war and did not go and knows I did and pretends he doesn't care. In this way we continue the game, the one in our sweaty heads, the other, the frisbee, which arcs like a rocket between us.

Jack is built like an iron bull. His broad shoulders frame a massive chest with twin pectoral shields; he is narrow-waisted; his abdomen is a ladder of muscle. His arms and legs are taut and firm. A square jaw juts a manly cleft chin. Beneath the pummeling sun his steely eyes glow in their sockets. He is fast, agile, cat-like.

Jack has smoked and drank and worked his body for ten years and today the red dragon tattoo which spans his proud chest breathes salty fire in the hot, sweet air.

We are standing fifty meters apart. When Jack wings the frisbee it cuts a well-placed bullet path into my waiting hands. My hands which are bleeding and blistered.

"Nice throw," I say.

Jack is astonished when I pivot and catch the energetic disk behind my back. He cannot believe it. I am ten years his senior. But I have killed, saved and lost men. I have the papers and medals to prove it.

Poor Jack. Poor well-built, swagger-walk, shaven-head, glow-eyed, stoned-cold Jack cannot believe my prowess.

"You're damn good," he says. "You're really damn good."

When I toss the dancing circle so well, so finely placed he need not move, not budge, not shift one inch to catch it, he is doubly astonished.

"Christ," he says.

Here is how we met:

The speed boat from Phnom Penh to Angkor Wat cost twenty-one dollars and took five hours. Inside, the long sleek craft is crowded with double rows of tourists. Many are drunk. They laugh, sing, and frolic. Others are sleeping, lulled by the constant roar of the boats turbo engines. I am kept awake by loud speakers hooked to the walls which blare American rock music throughout the stuffy cabin. After an hour the noise makes me crazy. I walk up a narrow stairway and sit in one of two canvas chairs near the stern. The boat scuds forward on the Tunnele Sap River; its pitch-dark water sprays my body and pelts my face. It feels good to be alive.

Soon another passenger, Jack, joins me. Bare chested, he is wearing military ripstop cargo pants. His blond hair is cut short and white-walled. As he walks the boat's roof he instinctively sways with the watery rhythm. By the way he steps, by the way he seats himself, drops his lean body into the sun-bleached chair, he exudes confidence. He exudes manliness. I do not ask about the furious dragon with its rolling eyes and scaly skin and whip like tail. After a time we speak.

"Yes, yes. I look too young but I was there and war is a terrible thing. It plays tricks on your mind," I say. "It changes you. But now we're in Cambodia and it's 1995." When I become emotional Jack looks away. Then I regain my poise and he tells me his story.

Jack enlisted in 1976 after one year of college. Infantry. Jump school. Special Forces. "Why?" I ask. Jack says his brother lost both legs in Vietnam. "Both legs," he repeats. Jack wanted revenge, but the Army said no. After a time he re-trained as a cook, and never left Ft. Carson.

For three years Jack griddles stuffed omelets, molds pastries, fancy breads, extracts the blood from immense raw steaks. For three long years he is undone by the clatter of cups, the clink of dishes, by white linen draped over smooth wood tables. Off duty he immerses himself in karate. He learns to kill with one punch and during this time seeks conflict in dark GI bars and bright public places. He is arrested many times. He has never lost a fight. When it is time to go he is honorably discharged with all rank and benefits despite his poor conduct. But Jack has obtained no medals, no battle scars, only minor bar room bruises. When I explain his good fortune Jack pretends to listen as the sea wind buffets our faces and cools our bodies.

As he tells me his story the hours pass and the boat slows

to enter a small narrow channel. Thin, tense Cambodian sailor's man American gun boats armed with heavy machine guns which are cocked and ready. The thin men come close then step aboard to inspect passenger documents.

"Pass-port. Pass-port," they say, stressing the syllables.

The Cambodians are wearing French camouflage uniforms and Chinese steel helmets. They carry AKs and M-16s and smooth American grenades. Frags, we called them. Some passengers take pictures but the sailors shoo them away, as if they are scolding children. Then the sailors are gone. When our boat pulls to shore we are met by a legion of nervous soldiers who form a phalanx through which we pass.

It begins raining a cold, piercing rain which turns the dark earth to chill muddy soup. The passengers, mostly young foreign backpackers freighted with too much clothing and gear slip and slide and look for shelter. Soon they panic. Only Jack and I remain calm. We make a gallant path through the fumbling amateurs. For some reason the frightened youth and well-armed men make way. We step with authority, we step forward as if we know this ground.

The driver of the idling truck is a middle-aged man, his caramel face pitted by a hundred stories that would take a lifetime to tell. He wears simple, common clothes; he wears a red-and-white checkered Cambodian scarf around his neck. When he speaks I watch the rise and fall of his jugular vein, which is thick with blood.

"Me take you to finest guest house," he says through a bridge of rotted teeth.

At first I never killed anyone. The machine gunners and riflemen did that. I carried morphine and bandages to ease their pain. The first dead American I saw was black. Then I helped in the killing. And the killing helped me.

It is cold and damp inside the rusting American military truck. Jack nods his approval. I lower my chin. There is war in my mouth and it tastes like bullets. I am silent. Then we are off. In the blinding downpour rain pelts the windshield in thunderous beats which makes sight impossible. I expect the last-minute swerve, the grind of gears, the screech of brakes, the slow motion fragmenting glass as our bodies pass through it. But the driver grips the wheel with one hand and repeatedly ducks his head out the side window, squinting and shaking and steering all at once. Soon he is thoroughly wet. Water drips round the sacred curve of his large Cambodian ears. It drips down the well-worn path made by his venerable cheek bones and triangular jaw. It drips into the red-white checkered scarf softly knotted around his throat. Water gathers and drifts down his lean torso, down his meager Asian hairless legs, down his delicate bare feet, until finally it pools itself onto the rotted steel floor and sinks to the flooded road beneath us.

In our wild dash through the broad and narrow streets of Siem Reap, as we glide and splash through submerged roads that crest like rivers, the pulsate drip, drip, drip of solitary water beads makes me calm.

"Here is guest house," says our driver, pointing toward a rain swept path.

We pay with wet money and rush outside. By the time we enter the clean, dry, well-lit room our clothes are drenched. Jack removes his shirt, seats himself at a wide yellow sofa, and busies himself in the crimp and curl of joints. I remain standing and silent and he thinks I'm strange. I say I'm cold and tired. I say perhaps tomorrow we'll visit Angkor Wat. Jack says "Sure" and I say good night. An ageless friendly woman emerges from a glass bead door. She parts it with her hands locked in prayer.

"Here key," she says, accepting money.

In my large room with its square thick bed and vault of mosquito netting I take pills and lie down and do not recall my dreams. Before sleep I tell myself I am good, I am calm, I am strong.

This is how it works: they walk into us, we walk into them, we walk into each other. Oh, there is magic in these moments. Magic in the mannered step of patrol, ambush, jungle, monsoon. Magic in the machine gun's vile abracadabra. Magic in the illusory arc of seamless tracers. Wizardry in the rampaging men who run, crouch, advance, explode. Oh, there is infinite wit and timely jest in the ten thousand ways men hunt and kill. Survival. That is the sacred trick of war. That is the heart of it. The obscene and secret center.

In the morning Jack and I flag down a weather-beaten motor cycle. It is a strange sight: two large men gathered around one thin man whose fragile machine we must commandeer to visit eternal Angkor Wat. In the banter of bargain the gaunt Cambodian stands his ground and we call his bluff by leaving.

"OK. OK," he shouts. "Five dollah for both. Five dollah."

A small fortune in a country where once a life could be lost for the crime of wearing glasses.

We straddle the slim seat and, bunched up, hold tight to flimsy belts.

"You ready? You ready?"

"Yes," we shout in unison.

The driver races down long empty boulevards flanked by massive leafy trees which make the morning air bright and cool. Only the sputtering engine breaks the invisible silence. Ghosts are nearby, I know it, I can feel them.

When we reach the great sprawling temple we are dumbstruck. The long pale building snakes across the horizon like a sideways totem spirit caught in the dream world between rest and waking. The strange organic stone palace beckons us forward. For three long hours we inhabit the intricate site. Stepping like deer over the white stone floors, we honor the warrior carvings. The driver grows impatient.

"All right," we say, and ride to a temple where the jungle has not been slashed and burned and cleared away.

"This Ta'Prom," says our driver. As we dismount he wipes sweat from his brow and beneath his breath utters the strange words "Khmer Rouge."

Jack tells him to wait by the side of the road and we begin walking forward. I look about. Where have I seen these great twisty vines, sky poking trees, dirt trails studded by jagged rocks cocooned in pillows of emerald moss? Where did I first hear the animate sounds of green triple canopy tranced with decay and life? I want to run, I want to hide, I want to plummet childlike into this vast room of living dreams.

But the sweltering heat makes us lazy. We drink rivers of bottled water and take refuge in lichen-covered stone temples where all colors are sublime. I sit and talk with a small boy selling souvenirs. Jack takes photographs, then hunkers down and smokes a paper stick while seated bunched up like a gargoyle.

Idiot, I want to say. We are guests to a lost age in sacred rooms which know the luminous voice of prayer and song. We are guests under low roofs locked in the vise of towering trees and serpentine vines. We are surrounded by stone and light and triple-layered jungle which knows no law but its own. Idiot, I want to say. Can you not feel each living moment tick past? Can you not know what it's like to live here? What it means to rush forward to the screaming men? Idiot, I want to say, can't you taste and smell the humans veiled in billowing cordite? Can't you see the frozen man who cannot move? In war the living become like statues lifted by helicopters, or left to decay. Silly, wasted idiot. Do you not know what it's like to wake from a monstrous dream still swallowed in sprawling nightmare?

See how the impartial sun fills me with fear. See how the percussive white hammer spits metal through skin. See how I freeze decades after the event.

Dear stoned wasted one: In war all suffer their fates. I am fortunate: The dead do not speak when I talk back. Or judge my sins. Look at you smoking your tight-rolled reveries. What do you know?

It is our third day at Angkor Wat. Jack knows I will meet

him later. I have risen early, hoisted my pack and sped to a deserted point behind Ta'Prom. In the lustrous emerald shelter I unfold the once-green nylon hammock still stained by red dirt. Automatically, my eyes measure the distance for its still strong rope. Automatically, my fingers loop square knots to the center of trees; my hands adjust the hammock to hang just above the ground, the better to roll out in case of attack. But there are only flies and leeches and the jungle's slow organic crawl. I smear insect repellent on my hands, on my arms, and face. I straddle the embracing nylon sheet, then sit, then lie straight back. I am running; I am hiding; I am plunging full force into the dream. The book I have brought falls from my hand.

At dusk, after we form a perimeter with trip flares, dig fox holes, plant mines, after we have eaten, after we have checked our weapons, drawn match sticks for guard, I lay in a small area cleared with a knife borrowed from a friend who will die in two weeks. In the middle of night a new man nearly steps on my face. "You're guard," he says, setting the bulky radio down before disappearing into the inky black.

I crawl to the foxhole. Its warm wet walls are studded with quick cut roots which bleed clear sap. An hour goes by. A voice whispers over the radio, "If you're sitreps are negative break squelch twice." But my situation report is not negative. Twenty, thirty meters ahead I hear the soft graze of cloth on twigs. I hear the tell-tale rise and push of rubber sandaled feet on the green-matted jungle floor. Huddled down, I squeeze the detonator and the mine explodes. A great white flash and metallic bang fill the air. For a moment they are visible. Then there is running and small arms fire and someone explodes a second mine. Boom! Now they are screaming. The machine gunners seek out survivors. In the morning we find blood trails and human meat. Save for one they have dragged away their dead. The frail human sculpture trapped in rags is riddled with bullets. The pith helmet beside her is torn to shreds. Her weapon is mangled and useless. It is she who wept and groaned all night; it is she whose pleading voice haunts us as we scavenge her pockets.

When I wake the sun is directly overhead. It is time to move out. Time to march to the field. I untie knots, coil the rope, spread the hammock flat on the ground, fold it lengthwise in half and roll it up, hoist my pack, and begin walking. It is a good twenty-minute hike on a well-used trail. The last three words have special meaning. I scan for footprints, heel marks dragged backwards. Automatically I bob and sway and keep to the side; I am searching for men who lie in wait. But there is nothing. Only the tranquil path and flitting birds and un-forbidding jungle. The mimic of memory. That is what most annoys me, what Jack cannot comprehend: When I see or smell or feel things, which are not there. For every step of the next mile I tell myself I am strong, I am calm, I am good.

"Christ," says Jack.

We continue playing. He whips the flying ring across the flat dead field. I catch it left-handed, or between my legs, or with eyes closed, whatever it takes to heighten the risk. The day burns bright with heat and I want to be ten thousand times more powerful than Jack, who grins at each weapon-like exchange. He presses a joint to his lips between turns. The plastic wheel sings like a bullet between us.

Suddenly behind Jack, nine young Cambodian troops emerge from the tree line. Their uniforms are ripped and filthy; their silent sandals are made from tires banded by strips of inner tube; tight-knotted red bandanas encircle their bushy heads. They wield a motley patchwork of AK-47s, shoulder-fired RPGs, a weary American machine gun. Yes. They have been hunting Khmer Rouge. Beads of sweat roll down their gaunt faces which they mop with the backs of their filthy hands. I watch as their black almond eyes track the dancing disk sweeping over the dry tan field. Their expression is unreadable.

Seeing a curious look on my face, Jack turns around.

After a moment he slings the frisbee to an older man who appears in charge. The man fumbles the catch and annoyed throws it back. It is a weak throw and he is clearly troubled. Jack laughs, then trots up to another soldier, man or woman it is hard to say, and offers the joint. The Cambodians uneasily share it, and Jack cannot control his laughter. He is slapping his sides. He is bent over double. In six puffs the paper wand evaporates but the Cambodians raise their weapons and point them at Jack. He finds this hilarious and laughs even louder.

Walking forward I stare straight into the Cambodians' blood raging eyes. Howling with laughter, Jack picks up the frisbee and tosses it to me. But I don't want to see it. Where are the foxholes? Where are the claymore mines? Where are the weapons and knives and radio? The war is everywhere and Jack is blind to it.

He continues to laugh. He thinks the forced grin on my face is reciprocal laughter. He thinks I have come to pick up the plastic wheel that has fallen at my trekking boot feet. He thinks I walk toward him and the seething group to triumph the joke in a halo of sweat. But when I reach Jack I throw the hardest punch of my life and he drops like a burlap bag filled with red dirt and does not move. Straightening up, I lock eyes with each Cambodian. The commander nods. The others lower their weapons. Then like mist they dissolve into the jungle.

I spoke to Jack as he lay there jaggedly jawed, the dead grass beneath him stippled red. Strange words flew from my mouth. I spoke non-stop and the words sounded fierce in a language I don't remember.

On the boat back to Phnom Penh I recalled the startled look in Jack's eyes. What had he seen and what did he know? Over the time it took to re-cross the Tunnele Sap I realized it didn't matter.

I continued traveling. Some days were good, some were bad. But I swear that I never, not once in all the hectic times that followed, whatever the country wherever I laid my head, did I ever look back. Like a river I am always moving forward.

The Most *&!% War Story Of %#*#! Time

Every third day Delta is re-supplied by Huey's which spot our popped smoke, swoop in, frantically unload crates of C-rations, ammo, mail, black rubber kegs of water, then they are gone.

The mail is stuffed in a red nylon sack tied shut with thick cotton rope. The lieutenant unties the bag, reaches in, dutifully hands out letters that bear name, rank, serial number, unit APO.

Teddy stares into space. "She's leaving me," he whispers.

Baker, ordered home on emergency leave, yells, "Fuckin A! I'm getting out!"

Ernie tears opens a parcel sent by his dad. He reads aloud the titles on the Red Cross cassette: "Side One: Trains Entering Station. Side Two: Trains Departing Station. Always love my choo-choo's," says this man unfit for combat.

Jim receives an Easter basket filled with fake grass and yellow marzipan eggs.

"Nothing for you, Doc," says the lieutenant.

What remains in the red sack are books and magazines: *Time, Reader's Digest, Popular Mechanics.* I grab a paperback by Jan Yoors, who has lived with gypsies. Check my watch. In an hour we'll move out, march through jungle, at dusk set up a perimeter. I write to the maker of salt tablets. I've written many such letters; it helps pass the time.

Dear Sir or Madam, Did the artist Gervasio Gallardo draw the cover for Peter S. Beagles' latest book? It's very beautiful. I intend to read the story when circumstances permit. Your reply is most appreciated.

Dear Sir or Madam, I would like to know what is meant by "process cheese."This term appears on the list of ingredients of your fine dairy product, which I enjoy immensely when not otherwise engaged.

There is time for a letter home.

Dear Folks, Today we killed five. They walked into our booby trap. They scream a lot. Then they are dead. The lieutenant says I'm doing good. The others do the killing. I'm the medic. So far I've patched up six guys. We're lucky. Been killing more than they kill us. Nobody understands how they don't bleed much. Can't figure it out. Gonna send something taken off a dead man. Keep it in a safe place. More when it happens. Love.

After an hour's march we stop, stake the trips and claymores, dig foxholes. Soon the skin mags circulate. I'm sitting next to the captain. We call him six.

"Sir, isn't she beautiful?"

I tear the centerfold from its stapled spine.

"I mean isn't she fuckin gorgeous?"

The kneeling buxom brunette has smooth sexy thighs; she has perfect pouting lips. As she leans forward her full American breasts spill from the page.

"Whatever you say, Doc."

Six grabs the handset from the RTO, calls in grid coordinates, our casualties, our body count. Stares at his topo map.

"Whatever you say."

It's my fourth month in country. Letters and parcels, books and magazines, all help take our minds off the clockwork of killing time or being killed.

There are not enough machetes for each man to clear a patch of jungle, stomp ants and insects, then hunker down until guard. Men write home for the long blades, for Marine K-bars, pistols, liquor, the damnedest things. Those who have lost hope do not write at all.

I tear a page from Popular Mechanics. Beneath the photo the ad screams: **ARMY SURPLUS KNIFE AND GENUINE LEATHER SCABBARD $4.95 + SHIPPING AND HANDLING. SUPPLIES LIMITED. THIS OFFER WILL NOT BE REPEATED.** But of course it is. Every month. Like clockwork. I clip the coupon.

Dear Mom and Dad, Today the Captain gave each medic a Bronze Star. He says we are good soldiers. He says this war will not last long. I need a favor. Pay these people. They'll send me the knife. I'll pay you back. Love.

I should have known better. She had her first breakdown in '65; soon afterward he had electric shock treatment. But I need them. Need their help.

It's been three weeks. Why haven't you answered my letter? Here's another coupon. Just send the fuckin knife. Your son, the medic.

When we are not hunting or being hunted I learn to Increase My Word Power, solve Brain Teasers, memorize Quotable Quotes, join the Rosicrucians, receive the cover art of *The Last Unicorn.* "Yes, Gervasio Gallardo was the artist," writes a Bantam Books editor. A week later a company in New York sends a typed note which solves the riddle of process cheese. There is a letter from home.

Everyone here is fine. The weather is wonderful. Uncle William says hello. Your father and I thought about the knife. We don't think it's a good idea. It's very sharp and you might hurt yourself. Write soon. X X X X X Mom & Dad.

Later I'll take a hand forged machete from a dead woman, strap it to my ruck, use it wisely. Years later, when I sleep with a loaded pistol under my pillow my college roommates think I'm crazy. In New York's Chinatown I buy a meat cleaver; for six years keep it near my bed. If there is noise at night I grab the handle, rise up, prowl soft footed, eager to strike. And later still, in Guatemala I buy a peasants' machete, carry it through Mexico, spirit it through Customs, tuck it half way beneath my New England mattress. But for now I go quietly berserk.

Winter: Uncle William sits with us at the dinner table. We have finished the meal, I have told the story and Uncle roars with such laughter that tears streak his face. "Why that's the stupidest war story of all time," he says. But Mother and Father are puzzled. "Why is he laughing? What's so funny?" they ask. Uncle William wipes his mouth, he swallows hard, then explains the tale I do not often tell.

The Thing They Will Always Carry

VA Shrink: Were you in Vietnam?
Vietnam Vet: Yes.
VA Shrink: When were you there?
Vietnam vet: Last night.

I'm kneeling. Tears streak my face, drip down, fall to earth. It's only my second time in combat. Soon I'll be different. Soon revenge for our dead and wounded will meld with fear and I will help with the killing and the killing will help me. We're just regular grunts: we make too much noise, we have no special skills, we're not elite. But after a time we get the hang of this war, the rhythm of it. Wait. Engage. Disengage. We call it contact or movement. "Bringing scunnion," we say. We psych ourselves up with, "Time to kick ass and take names." And between contact and kicking ass or having our asses kicked there is tension that starts small, then builds and builds until we secretly pray it will happen. That we walk into them or them into us, or we mortar them or they rocket us, then the tension explodes like perfect sex, and afterwards, we're spent. There are days, weeks when nothing happens, then terror, instant and deep, then relief, like paradise, since the killing is done and we've buried away the wounded and dead. Until it starts all over again.

That was thirty-seven years ago. Or was it last night? A day, a year, twenty years home from war and you may begin to act strange. The shrinks and social workers, the clinical researchers, each has a different take on what causes PTSD. "It's neuro-linguistic. It's cognitive. It's biochemical," they chime and chatter. Who cares? Just stop the pain. Just stop it. But where does that pain come from? What's going down?

Here is what I know: What you learn in combat you do not easily forget. You drop at the first hint of an ambush falling so fast your helmet still spins in the air. You shoot first and ask questions later. The enemy is an unfeeling slippery bug to be stomped out. You live like an animal. You learn to like killing. Learn to fear and hate the enemy. Hate civilians. Can't trust the bastards. You hate taking prisoners. You'd rather kill them. Why? Because the enemy wants to fuck you up. Kill you, your pals, some new guy doesn't know jack shit, wants to waste your lieutenant, the whole damn platoon.

After a time you learn what war is: the fish like iridescent gleam inside a brainless head; the sleek pink caterpillar of pulsing human gut; the grotesque tableau of charred bodies frozen stiff; the impossible music made by voices howling beyond human form; pure white bones piercing ruby ripped flesh; the strange oily feel of fresh human blood; the sudden slump of the man next to you. And always, the business of flies on the mouths of the dead.

After a time, to a supernatural degree you learn to live with terror, rage, struck down sorrow, blocked out guilt or dumbstruck grief. Yes, the supernatural threat of catastrophe and the ways to survive it become preternaturally normal, second nature, a fully formed part of you.

Then one day you get shot, or if you are lucky, complete the tour, return home intact. But for those who have seen their share the equation might go like this: Johnny got his gun + Johnny marches home = HEEEREE'S JOHNNNNY!!!!

And the good soldier John or the good troop Jane, who under fire never once thought of your silly civil rights, your silly little flag, your doofus politics, Good Johnny or Jane, I say, feel and act a tad differently when the locked down feelings, the bottled up memories, the instinctive behaviors of Post-Traumatic Stress Disorder fervently, unexpectedly, kick in. The symptoms of PTSD, in plain bloody English, are as follows:

Flashbacks: reliving a combat event as if it were happening to you right now.

Hypervigilance: to be always on guard, always looking or listening for where the next shot, the next grenade, next rocket, ambush or IED will come from.

Survivor guilt: feeling bad, feeling real shitty for having lived when others in the squad or platoon got killed.

Moral Guilt: wrestling with actions you did or didn't take that resulted in someone getting seriously fucked up. Or you saw something truly awful that is seriously off the charts.

Startle Reflex: dropping, flinching, turning fast at a sudden noise or unexpected touch.

Suicidal Ideation: thinking about killing yourself.

Homicidal Ideation: thoughts about killing people. Strangers, friends, it doesn't matter.

Homicidal Rage: anger way out of proportion to an everyday event. It comes quick, down and dirty. You want to do major damage because of something trivial.

Nightmares: violent dreams often related to combat. Sometimes it's the same dream. You moan or talk in your sleep, thrash in bed, wake up scared or sweaty. Sometimes you hit grab or hit the person beside you.

Ritual Behavior: at night, before going to sleep, you check the lights, lock the doors, maybe keep a weapon at hand. Some vets call this 'walking the perimeter.'

Alienation: feeling as if no one understands you. Feeling like you don't fit in with your pals or the public. Feeling like you should never have come home.

Panic Attacks: a short and sudden and intensely fearful state of mind. Some vets sweat or breathe hard, or have a pounding heart, or get dizzy or choke.

Social Isolation: Being alone for long periods of time. In public, your friends think you're strange and strangers think you're dangerous because you hardly ever talk.

Drug and alcohol abuse: whatever works to dull the pain inside your head.

Fear of Emotional Intimacy: many combat vets can't or won't allow anyone to get emotionally close to them. If someone tries, the vet may back off or ignore the advance or push the perceived threat away.

Employment: A lot of vets can't keep a job. Every couple of months they quit or are fired.

Psychic Numbing: The inability to feel emotions. Vets describe it as feeling hollow, empty, blank.

Denial: Problems? What problem? I don't have a fuckin' problem!

High Risk Behavior: Gambling, driving too fast, whatever it takes to relive the rush of combat.

Sadness, Depression, Anxiety, Crying Spells.

These symptoms are normal responses to extraordinary events outside the range of normal human experience. Most American's no nothing of war and even less of its aftermath.

Some types of treatment: The talking cure: a vet talks to a therapist who is skilled in treating war stress. There are many techniques. In Immersion therapy, a vet is asked to remember a traumatic event, progressing from less painful to very painful thoughts in order to overcome ideas and feelings which prevent healthy behavior. Cognitive behavioral therapy seeks to challenge and replace unhealthy patterns of thought. In group therapy, seven to ten vets meet once a week for an hour or two. A experienced group leader is essential. That person knows when to talk, when to listen, and how to keep the group focused. EMDR is a type of hypnosis in which the vet, fully awake, may experience relief from buried trauma. MDMA/Ecstasy, has been clinically proven to help vets with PTSD. The drug Ketamine shows much promise.

In addition: Exercise, meditation, yoga, prescribed meds, an artistic endeavor, a friend who will listen. Whatever works that does no harm. Know that many vets fear talking about their combat experiences. They dread losing control. They dread looking weak or vulnerable. They fear the act of crying.

My advice to you who've been to war up close and personal: find a way to face your dread, your fears, your shame and sorrows. Chances are good that over time you will live less in the past, more in the present, but you will never be the same. WWII, Korea, Panama, Vietnam, Iraq, Afghanistan, Central America, Africa: Wherever you were, whatever you did in war will always be with you. Always.

When He Was Good

Martin stood in the parking lot. The black asphalt shimmered like tarmac on chopper pads. Annette was late. When her Land Rover pulled in he called to her.

"Looks like a tank," he said, then smartly opened the door, settled himself, kissed her extended cheek.

"Lovely day," said Annette. "Isn't it gorgeous?" her British accent ever fresh and new. Martin winked at her. She slipped her right hand from the clutch to his thigh, then back, pulled into traffic.

"Right, then. Happy to see me?"

He leaned over and kissed the shaded cleft behind her right ear.

"You're such a naughty boy, aren't you?" she said.

Annette fiddled with the radio, searched for music, news, anything.

"That's fine," said Martin. "Right there."

He flexed his body in time to the pumping beat, eyed her blouse, the inviting curve of her breasts. Annette was not pretty, he thought; her features were tight, drawn, severe, as if she were a salmon after the run up river.

"Sometimes I think you work too hard," he said.

"Really? But you do put up with all my sass."

"I figured you'd call sooner or later," said Martin. "I missed you," he said, fingering the clefts between her knuckles as if they were his own.

"I read all your letters," she said. "I was absolutely delighted...delighted by what you wrote." She turned to him. "Sexual love is...is so much easier to sustain, don't you think?"

She snared his hand in hers, then turned the radio mute. He smiled at the distorted reflection of himself dancing in the opaque lens of her sunglasses.

"Frankel says there are three kinds of love. Impersonal, personal and irreplaceable," he replied.

The light changed. Annette accelerated, overtaking a rumbling tractor trailer.

"Did I tell you my neighbors' tree smashed into the side of my house last night? He had the nerve to say it was my fault. Mine!"

She swerved into the fast lane.

"Did anyone get hurt?" asked Martin.

He spooled the volume dial clockwise.

Annette turned right on Warton Street; a parade of ornate homes and well-kept lawns soldiered into view.

"Oh, have a look. Have a look," she chortled, pulling up the driveway. "The workmen were here." She pointed to the dismembered tree, its trunk and branches neatly stacked to one side. "You're so lucky no one was injured," she mimicked, tugging back the emergency brake. "Well, now," she said, parting her legs to exit the vehicle. "Have a look at my lovely garden!"

Stepping out, Annette pinched the remote alarm on her key chain. The horn beeped once. Martin thought it sounded like a metal goose shot in the wing.

"It's the deer," she said, pointing to the wilted stalks and bald patches of earth. "They come down from the reservation. I've called our bloody Mayor twice, and I said to him, 'Julian, those animals are positively ruining my land. You absolutely must set out poison or have the hunters in.' He said he'd look into it." Annette nodded to the land and looked at him mournfully. "Now this."

Martin estimated the garden measured ten meters by twelve; the backyard, one acre. Trees and shrubs edged the sides of her property. There was no fence to ward off intruders. A Victorian house peeked through a line of sycamores thirty meters away. He noticed the deer tracks, pouted and frowned, then stepped behind her, embraced her body, nuzzled her neck.

"It looks different," he said, pointing past the ominous tree line.

"Oh, that," she said. "They painted it last week." Annette dug her backside into his groin. "I rather liked it when it was blue. Now it's just... Oh, I don't know...who would ever paint their house solid red? Can you image..."

Martin closed his eyes, saw the pith helmeted blur figures running past. His neck snapped left to right.

"...or suppose they installed one of those dreadful mosquito killing machines?" She paused. "Are you alright, darling?"

"Yes, everything is under control."

Martin began to undo the hard plastic buttons of Annette's blouse. He dipped his fingers inside, toyed with her lacy bra, dotted the nape of her neck with kisses until she quivered. Annette turned round and faced him.

"You naughty, naughty man. In front of my nosy neighbors, will you? Inside, or I shall have to call the police!"

To quiet her, Martin pressed a soft, luxuriant kiss to her mouth.

"Fancy something to eat?" she asked.

"Maybe later. I need to work up an appetite."

"You rascal. Come with me."

Annette took him by the hand as they walked from the well-appointed kitchen, its walls hugged by a forest of gourmet utensils hung from dainty hooks, to the immense living room. A hand frosted bay window overlooked the broad lawn and narrow cobble stoned street. Tall gas lanterns were posted every hundred meters.

"Isn't it just lovely?" she said, gesturing to an exquisite glass table and leather-bound chairs, a black plush sofa, an array of exotic wall hangings and marble statues. "Mum left it to me. None of it's really mine. Well, I suppose it is." She planted her fortyish chin to an upturned palm.

"How old was she?" asked Martin.

"Nearly ninety," she said. "I never told you? 'I simply must have my own bed and bath, Annette. Really. How perfectly dreadful, those horrid American elder farms.' Elder farms! Dear Lord."

"Do you miss her?"

Martin drew her hand away from her face and thumbed the curve of her mouth.

"Good gracious, no," she said. "Nothing ever suited Mum, darling. Nothing. But...all that's past now." She led him forward. "What do you think? Charming, isn't it?"

On one side of the room two bookcases stood packed with grade school reference books, assorted toys and games, each item tucked precisely in place. He imagined not one item missing.

"Very nice," he said, fingering the well-worn spines.

"Those are my favorites," she said, pointing to an orderly shelf crammed with jigsaw puzzles. "I absolutely adore them. Sometimes the girls and I spend hours on the silly things... Don't look so sad," she teased, looking past him.

Stepping forward, Annette pushed Play. The blinking answering machine whirred to life. A young man's voice, coy and energetic, spoke.

"Hi. It's me. Wondering when we can spend time together. I've been working out...hard. I think you'll like what you'll see. Tomorrow I have tickets for..."

"Oh, you and your bloody tickets," Annette shouted, shutting off the machine.

He knew of her lovers. Once, she had written him: As to my young stallions, well, in fact, how shall I say this, here is one chap I am rather fond of. We tryst weekends, when the kiddies are with their Dad. And, well, dammit, yes, there is a youngster I occasionally visit, a client, but it's simply puppy love, darling. At least Frederick is gone. The bastard. Martin, I will not be intimate with these two any longer if we have a go at it."

He thumbed a shelf full of encyclopedias; below it, a tin-cased biology set complete with specimens and microscope. Two adult frogs, vacuum packed in formaldehyde stared at him, their large black eyes unblinking.

"I thought you weren't seeing him anymore."

"It's nothing...nothing, I assure you, sweetheart. Can you believe he sent me flowers, with a card, handwritten by the florist, for God's sake. 'To my busty Brit. Love, Kisses, Yours ever so deeply, Robert.' Bastard!"

" 'I'm whole again," he said, reading from a sheet of torn paper found wedged in Volume Seven, Renaissance Literature and Art. "'Harpooned by a doctor yesterday. He slipped an illuminated plastic eel down my KY jellied cock and determined I will need only minor surgery. This is good news, dear Annette. The procedure will not incapacitate my ability to make a certain woman ooze with delight. Yours sincerely, Martin.'"

"Whatever will I do with you?" she said, re-buttoning her blouse.

He took her hand away and held it. She continued to speak, her voice trailing after him as they walked up the spiral staircase to her bedroom.

It was their tenth meeting in four months. This time he hoped things would be different. Her response to his personal ad had been straightforward and provocative. "What I wouldn't give for a good and virile lover. Whatever is one to do? Have any ideas? Yours, A." But their encounters were flaccid, uninspired, boring. She had no sense of play: Sex was a business deal to be discreetly obtained and off shore harbored, her executive orgasms a curated series of stifled yelps and well-mannered postures. He wished she would just once relax and let him make love to her.

Hand lightly tapping the staircase banister, he imagined her slowly undressing in front of him, heard the soft rustle of silk against her lambent skin, her blouse and skirt falling to the hardwood floor. "Leave your shoes on," he would say, and watch as she unclasped the lacy bra, slowly unshouldered it and leaned forward, her nipples erect, her full breasts plump and radiant. "Look what she's done now," said Annette, sweeping her hand across the room. "I've told Dolores a dozen times, solid color sheets on Monday. Solid. Honestly..."

He shrugged.

"Right then."

She kicked off her shoes, undressed quickly, folded her clothes over the back of an antique chair, then slipped into bed, not once looking at him.

"It's a gun," said Martin, leaning over her, hoping she would tease his pleasure.

She looked up and frowned.

"You know I don't go in for that sort of thing. Besides, the children will be back from school at three thirty. It isn't as if we had all day, darling." She lowered the covers, her body a target. "You do understand, don't you? Say yes."

Unzipping himself, he took her right hand and guided it between his legs.

"You devil," she said, fondling him.

Martin undid his belt, uncoupled his pants, let them drop to the floor. Annette pulled his briefs down.

"Good Lord!" she said, reluctantly drawing him to her mouth.

"Slowly," he said, watching her lips encircled him. He traced delicate patterns around her ears while shifting her head back and forth.

"My turn," she said. "You're on top. Come along, darling. Well, come on."

Annette threw herself back, parted her legs and waited.

Martin sheathed himself. Embracing her, he gently pulled himself inside, pinned Annette down, pushed softly, then hard, then plunged himself full forward into her body.

"You...you demon!" she stammered. "Wherever did you learn that?

"Shhhh..." he said, prompting her legs around him. She tried moving her hips in time with his. Turning sideways, he guided her, suckled her breasts, kissed her, gripped her buttocks, felt the tingling sensation begin.

"Slowly..." he whispered, and tried to think of other things.

Annette was driving; traffic lights blinked red-green-red. She eased the huge car into the driveway, carried on about her garden, the foliage; he glimpsed the village beyond the wood line, heard men run past, smelt the foul enemy scent, shook as machine guns fired, flinched as the wounded screamed: Am I alright, Doc? Am I alright? How bad is it? How bad?

Beneath him, her body arched and trembled; her lips formed an involuntary exit for the moaning sound. He watched her jaw clamp shut, stunting the pleasure. He groaned. They slept.

Annette kissed him awake, short, lackluster pecks on one side of his face. It had happened again. The frustrated love making; the war inescapable.

"Well, aren't you the quiet American," she snickered.

He remained motionless.

"Are you alright, sweetheart?"

She fluffed her pillow as though spanking a child.

"I was thinking of something. Would you like to hear it?" he asked.

"Oh, bloody hell, why not?"

Curling up next to him, Annette twirled the hairs on the back of his neck. Martin nearly turned to kiss her.

"It's always good to travel in pairs," he said. "Backpacking. Ever done that?" He nibbled her hand.

"All that muck and filth? Good heavens, no."

He continued speaking.

"We found a cheap place with an air conditioner, flush toilets, mosquito nets..."

"Mosquitoes? Where on earth were you?"

"I'm getting undressed, Alex is stepping out of the shower, towel wrapped around him, in walks this girl. 'Boom boom? You want boom boom?' "

Annette lifted her head from the pillow, slapping the bed as she spoke.

"What the bloody hell is 'boom boom'?"

"Sex," he said.

"Really? What kind of people would call the most intimate expression between two people boom boom? Dear God, that's absolutely horrid."

Laying back, she caressed him.

"The Americans," he said.

"And how would you know?"

She stretched with anxious pleasure.

"We spoke that way during the war," he murmured, wondering why he had told her.

She paused, eye brows knotted in puzzled concentration.

"Not that awful mess..."

He trailed his fingertips up the length of her arm.

"She was pretty. Better looking than the woman in Phnom Penh."

"Goodness, you do get around, darling. Isn't that the capitol of..."

"Cambodia," he said, recollecting the event.

They had choppered into an enemy base camp. No one expected to live.

"In June we were over run," he heard himself whisper.

Annette drew his hand to her breast, at the same time turning opposite, her backside pressed against his cock, making it large.

"Well, don't stop now, darling. This is absolutely

67

delightful!"

He felt blood rush to his face.

"She wanted ten dollars," he said. "A lot of money for not getting laid."

"What on earth?" she shrilled with excitement.

"They have a problem with HIV," he said, and felt her stomach tighten. "Alex got dressed and went out for a walk. We bargained in sign language."

He flashed the fingers of his right hand directly over her head.

"You beast, you absolute Minotaur!" Annette shrieked. "Go on! Oh, do go on!" she squealed.

The girl had kicked off her clogs and perched on the spring coil bed, squatting Viet Cong style. He pantomimed; her blouse fell to the floor.

"She didn't understand," he said, tracing a phantom arc of confused and awkward movements in the space between them. "Pulled and pushed my cock every which way."

Perplexed, the girl had closed her eyes, making her more beautiful.

"It was awful."

Annette shook with laughter.

"Oh, darling! You are absolutely precious! A hand job was it?"

She wailed with delight.

"I had to show her," he said.

His voice was not pleasant.

Annette curled the O shape of her thumb and forefinger around his swollen cock.

"Like that?" she asked, child-like.

"Yes. Like that."

Martin kissed her harshly on the mouth.

"This is brilliant...brilliant! Oh, go on! Go on!"

He pushed her tight clenched fist away.

"I stopped her," he said. "Just held her in my arms. Even travelers get lonely. Know what I mean?"

"Are you trying to tell me something, darling? Don't you think I'm sexy? Well? Don't you?"

She was impossible.

"Maybe. Maybe not."

Annette wagged a school marm's finger in Martin's face. He swatted it back.

"What then, darling?" she tittered.

"What then?" he mimicked. "I kissed her breasts, her mouth, pinched and rolled her nipples between my fingers until they were hard. You should have seen the look on her face, the way her eyes lit up."

He had held her close, smoothed and kissed her hair. She had spoken to him while dreaming.

"Well don't stop!" Annette commanded. "What happened next? Oh, do tell! Do tell!"

Hours later, in the musty bathroom they had showered and toweled each other dry. Dressed, they went out to eat.

"You-good-me," she had said.

That night he bought clothes for her children.

"So the little bitch couldn't wank you!" Annette crowed.

He shrugged indifferently.

"Oh darling, this is priceless. Better than Waugh... than Lawrence. Have you read them? Surely you've read Frank Harris?" She paused. "Darling, did you ever see her again?"

"No," he said, turning away.

"Well, after all...she was just a tart," Annette stammered, "A slut, really. It was business, for God sake."

For several minutes they lay without moving. Martin watched the second hand of the bedside clock swerve past the illuminated roman numerals. The memory always stopped at the clouds of smoke spewed by their weapons. Ten lay where they fell, bodies perforated, the agony having lasted all night. Sometimes the scream sounds made him weep. A machine gun burst decapitated one survivor. The lieutenant shot the other at close range. He saw it clearly now. The platoon scavenging the dead for souvenirs. The woman moved, her uniform spattered in brain and blood. She groaned, then raised a feeble arm, clawing at his canteen. The others bickered how best to kill her. He knelt down and tipped the plastic jug to her broken lips, watched as she suckled herself back to life. He shielded his eyes so they would not see.

Still blinking, Martin removed the wet hands from his face. Annette stared at him; wordless sounds spilled from her mouth. Except for his lowing sobs, which rattled and shook both their bodies, for a very long time they did not move.

The Exit Stage

It is 1971. A cold year. Heavy with snow, bitter with rain. It is one year since the killing time, when men fell like red drops in a bad storm and their thunderous screams filled day and night. It is the time before nightmares. It is the time before furious sex. It is the time before the rising rage. It is the time before doctors pushed drugs which only made me shake. It is the time before a car killed my dog and I wept, unable to bring her back; it is the time before the days of drink; it is the time before lawless deeds. It is the time before walking up to hollow-eyed men, asking, "Who were you with? What year?" It is the time before regretting I did not shoot the officer who tried to send me back on patrol. A mistake, he said, hands raised, my weapon trained on his chest. It is the time before moving sixteen times in less than one year. It is the time before I pressed unloaded pistols to young girls' heads. It is the time before the time when life is neither good nor bad. It is the time before I understand human beings.

It is Friday. I work six days a week. I am the head doorman at the Branford Theater in Newark, New Jersey. Outside, in the sleeting cold, large black letters hung on a triangular marquee tout the feature films, their ratings and times.

Shivering customers huddle beneath the illuminated tent. They wait to buy cardboard tickets from a young girl enclosed in a cramped black booth. One at a time they push their money under a metal grill. The girl mechanically presses a large green button, makes change, counts it twice, then pushes the ticket and money back into their shivery hands. One by one the customers push past thick wood doors located behind the booth. They walk, or amble, or strut down the well-lit corridor, which is fifty meters long, mirrors flanking either side. The people walk towards me.

It is the time before computers. It is the time before automatic inventory control. It is the time when hands still must do tedious things. Each ticket has a hole through its center. I slot the paper square onto a long thin rod centered in a sturdy, waist-high, rectangular, gray metal box. The ticket shimmies backwards down the upright pole. Later, the manager will loop black thread around the top of the over-sized needle. He will upturn the box, causing the tickets to form a bracelet of perforated squares. Behind locked doors he will count them one by one, just as he will count the paper cups, candy bars, hot dogs, and popcorn boxes, which remain after Irish Lucy, whose hair is a forest of fire, closes the glittery concession and hands him cash. Even though he trusts Lucy, by subtracting items remaining in stock the manager determines the day's take. The previous girl had skimmed the till, stashing her loot in garbage bags, which she later recovered in the alley way, out back. Confronted, she confessed, and was let go.

A set of double doors past the concession stand leads to the main auditorium. It can seat four hundred people. The cushioned chairs have small metal plaques nailed to the right armrest. Several seats have been stabbed or slit open. The yellow foam rubber puffs out like a rose bush in permanent bloom. Most chairs creak from age and abuse. The balcony, reached by a narrow staircase, can hold one hundred and twenty-five people. But there are rats and most customers sit elsewhere.

Intricate plaster designs and gold leaf trim cover the

theaters long high walls. An ornate chandelier hangs defiantly overhead. When the house lights dim, all eyes focus on the motorized velvet curtain, which raises in a series of reverse cascades like a maiden hoisting her skirts. As they watch the coming attractions customers munch or chew or lick their salty lips. Soon the lights will go out, the curtain will close and reopen and the main picture will begin.

Six days a week, eight hours a day, half hour lunch, wearing a black tuxedo, white shirt, bow tie, and shined black shoes, I take tickets.

"Tickets, please. Have your tickets ready. Tickets." No one knows I carry a gun.

Sometimes I flirt with pretty girls. Sometimes I let them in free. And sometimes I have interesting conversations with men. For example, one afternoon a middle-aged man spoke at length about Christ. Even Lucy listened to his impassioned appeals. But then his voice went wild and he spoke in tongues and the ushers came and threw him out. I had never seen that before. Speaking in tongues. Nor did I know what a bulldagger was until Lucy waited for the patron to leave. "It's a woman," she said. "They dress like that. They do sinful things. Sinful. Shame on them. Shame. Shame. Shame."

Lucy is slender, gaunt, bony and frail. Crimson spider veins flush her nose and cheeks. She is old. Perhaps fifty. Perhaps sixty-five. Her long bad teeth jut forward when she opens her mouth. When customers ask, Lucy names each item for sale. Names and prices. She does this a hundred times a day. I hate when she does it. The same words over and over. The same uncaring tone in her voice. Lucy wears too much make up. She looks as if she wears a mask. A scarlet mask, like a sneering devil or mocking clown, a painted whore, which makes me mad.

Whenever I speak or listen to Lucy I look at the space between her eyes, the one just above her delicate nose. In this way I make no true eye contact, though like most people she thinks I do. Otherwise Lucy will look like a woman before her husband and daughter and three sons have been shot. Otherwise I might scream at Lucy to shut the fuck up, butt stroke her across her red flushed face. And Lucy will drop silly and not feel the blows of our boots, as they, too, are covered in the color I hate.

I forget why it happened. Hector is different. He is young, mustachioed, handsome. He parts his straight black hair high on the right side of his head. With his thin waist, dark eyes, and sharp, angular features he reminds me of Mendez, met on the long, crowded flight departing the faraway land.

With his three Silver Stars and two Purple Hearts, Mendez the medic unleashed harrowing tales until he slumped down, drunk on gin, covered in ghosts. Like Mendez, I was a medic. We loved our men. When the airplane lands, Mendez holds me close in the arc of his arms. Holds me until the shaking stops. I have missed the closeness which comes with combat. Today, I do not know something of Hector and wish to know it. We talk secret, and when Lucy leans to our moving mouths, she cannot hear us.

"One o'clock," I say. "By the balcony exit."

I take his ticket and watch it sail down the sturdy pole. When I look up, another customer awaits.

Two hours later I unlock a service door and lead Hector up the fire escape to a large storeroom. Its high brick walls hold large thick windows embedded with steel thread to make them safe. Wide shafts of sunlight filter into the room, illuminating the dust our steps kick up. We look about. Cleaning supplies, dry stiff mops and rusty buckets crowd the walls. Wooden ladders lack pivotal slats. Below us, as the movie unfolds the loud speakers make the floor tremble. But inside the sun-lit room it is quiet.

Like boxers squaring off we stand one meter apart, ready to strike. With my right hand gripping the loaded twenty-five automatic pistol sheltered in my coat pocket I wait for Hector to suck my cock. If he makes one wrong move I will shoot him. Yes. Although I have never had a man suck my cock, I will shoot Hector if he takes one false step. I have done that. And I know that seeing and touching and smelling the dead is better than sex, and killing is even better.

Hector says, "C'mon man. Do it."

I say, "I thought you were doing me."

I say to myself, 'Careful. If he makes one false move shoot him. Shoot the fucker.'

Hector drops to his knees, unbuttons my pants, unzips my fly, and smothers my cock with his mouth. After a time I grow big watching his head bob like a piston forward and back. He is very excited. After a time he works up a lather of white spittle which coats the length of my cock. His mouth glides over the slippery foam.

I have fear. I fear spit has forever saturated my cock. I fear my cock is ruined.

After a time, discreetly aiming the gun at his head I say, "That's enough, Hector. I don't want anymore."

Hector continues a moment, then stops.

I say, "We have to go."

Still on his knees, Hector says, "Take off your shirt, man. C'mon, drop your pants. I want to see you naked."

I unbutton my shirt and expose my chest.

"More," he says. "Back up. So I can see you."

I take three steps back and feel the sun on my neck. I open my shirt. My loosened tuxedo pants fall to the floor. My body is still lean and muscular from jungle patrols. For several minutes I stand nude for handsome, smooth-talking, cock-sucking, spic-faced Hector. But if he takes one wrong step I will draw my weapon and shoot. The small bullet will penetrate his brain and he will be dead. Yes. I will shoot and kill this black-haired, wheat-faced, spic-fuck, cock-sucking, fucker who has spoiled my dick. And I will curse and kick the round blue hole in his spic-fuck head. I will kill and kick the one who has spoiled my cock.

"Muy bonita," says Hector. *"Muy, muy bonita."*

I set the safety and put on my clothes.

At the exit landing, before we re-enter the theater, Hector says, "Don't tell anyone, all right?"

What the fuck? I am twenty-one years old. I have four confirmed kills. I fragged a lieutenant. I lost half my platoon. But Hector, whose slippery mouth and rapid tongue have searched and destroyed my unscathed cock says don't tell? What the fuck, over?

In my best combat voice, the one used to tell the stuck pig wounded they are all right, the one used to calm impossible pain, the one used to instill false hope, to calm other men, I say, "Don't worry. I won't tell."

Then he is gone.

Downstairs, I lock myself in the narrow employees' bathroom and repeatedly bathe and scrub and wash my dick with warm soapy water. When I am satisfied it is clean, restored, safe, I return to work.

Lucy, who has covered for me, says, "You're late."

Straightening my jacket and pants, arranging my tie, I say, "It won't happen again."

I look down into the gray metal box. There are many tickets to count.

On the third day of the third month of 1971 I was fired from the Branford Theater. I have never married. I do not drink or smoke or use drugs. I have nightmares. I have crying spells. I spend much time alone.

And what of the Branford? Gone, whittled in half, the once-towering building now flat- faced with plate windows and white signs shouting impossible value. Inside, the bland interior is stocked with bins piled with failed merchandise. There is no mirrored corridor. There is no stairway. There is no second floor.

Gone too are the laughing children, drunks, pimps, cons, the lonely men and lonelier women. Gone are carpeted floors and heavy brass rails; gone the hidden projection booth and its slow whirring, two-reeled carbon arc projector run by a man whose name was Lee; gone are the velvet curtains, dimming lights and hundred-foot screen. Gone are the sudden gasps, shouted curses, cascading litter; gone are the trudging foot falls of satisfied patrons hurrying home before dark.

Nothing remains of the Branford Theater. Only the narrow, garbage-strewn alley out back escaped untouched. It is fenced off on both ends, locked tight, impossible to enter or exit. I once looked past the thick link chains and saw myself walking. The scent of stale urine seemed to rise over broken glass, crumpled cans; the sounds of stifled sex. I heard rats scurry in the shadows created by tall humming lamps which curved overhead. Further on, in dark forbidding spots I felt the hot breath of men lying in wait. I swore I saw blood. I swore I saw the surrendering man shot point blank. Everywhere I saw the blood of memory. I looked away. Nothing was left. Nothing.

And the gun?

Any automatic pistol has four main parts. Frame, slide, barrel, magazine. The practiced hand can break down and reassemble a pistol in thirty seconds. Twenty is better. And last summer, on a very hot day I pushed the safety on, depressed the magazine button, drew the slide back to inspect the chamber, removed the barrel from the slide by rotating it out, eased the slide off the frame and removed the recoil spring and guide bar from the frame tunnel. I did that. I've done it many times.

And after cleaning the weapon with poisonous solvent and soft round patches, after wiping it down, after applying a small amount of gun oil to each moving part, after reassembling the weapon, after inserting an empty ammo clip, retracting the slide, checking the breach, letting the slide snap forward, I pointed the slick, clean weapon upward and pulled the trigger one last time, the action sharp, smooth, tight, then put the gun away, hoping to never use it again.

Meeting The New Lieutenant

After eight months in the bush I say good-bye to the men. "Doc, don't leave us," they say, "Don't leave the platoon."

I don't want to leave. We have been through so much. Weeks on end of jungle patrols, sudden fire fights, the terror of rocket and mortar attacks. The dread night sappers overran our base. Or the endless waiting, the tension rising, and nothing would happen, nothing at all. In monsoon we lived and bled in mud and rain. In dry season slogged to the beat of our heated steps. And always they protected me. "Gotta keep you safe, Doc, you patch me up if I'm hit," said Wilson the RTO, piling on top moments before the Chicom exploded, everyone studded with shrapnel. Everyone but me. And always, at the sound of my name or the sight of their cuts and scratches, bloody leech bites, skin moldering ring worm, stinking jungle rot, their wild fevers, I cared for them. I always will.

Skinny Bob asks, "You're not really leaving, are you Doc?"

I clamp my jaw tight, crush the tears lodged in my throat. Skinny Bob is no longer the gangly, bad luck, won't live long FNG I nicknamed six months back. He is good in an ambush, on guard duty, patrols. But in two weeks, Skinny Bob, who I have learned to love, will be shot at close range and my replacement will not save him.

"Where to on R&R, Doc?" asks Big Ken, the likeable

giant who will die the same day, torn in two by machine gun fire.

"Japan," I mutter, and fib a smile to the men gathered round.

Someone asks, "Then what you gonna do?"

"Got a rear job in Phuc Vinh," I manage to say.

"We'll miss you, Doc. We'll miss you."

I don't want to leave them. But I've done eight months, it's time to leave the beautiful jungle, leave the forever fear and dread, say good bye, take the safe rear job with clean clothes, showers, real beds, reinforced bunkers, fresh food.

After handshakes and back slaps and secret tears, it's over. I'm out of the bush, a hundred times safer, one more step closer to home.

In Saigon, boarding a plane in civilian clothes, I feel naked without my M16, 45, frags, bandoliers, canteens. *Naked.*

I sit next to Spec 4 Samuel Chun, an upbeat well educated Japanese American. A clerk in Phuc Binh, he types finance reports. Not once during the six-hour flight does he use foul language.

From Tokyo we find our way to the Star Hotel.

"Good pussy and good dope," said Keifer, a medic in first platoon. "You'll have a great time.

Sam is agreeable, or so it seems.

Past the well-kept garden and its trickling fountain, past the white marble statue of plump happy Buddha guarding the oak front door, inside the boxy two story building, there are endless hallways with furnished rooms; all are empty and dark. Sam and I are the last Americans to visit this war time bordello. The owner, a plump elderly Mama-san, feigns eternal delight.

"Welcome. Welcome," she says, wiggling the fingers of both her hands.

At her side, Papa-san, a short gaunt fellow, who immediately tells us he fought in World War II.

"Mah-cheen-gun," he says, between bursts of smiles.

Mama-san cheerfully leads us to a ghost town of tables and chairs.

"Sit... sit," she says, pointing to a large black couch edging a deserted bar. She nods politely, then exits through a curtain of colorful beads, which continue to clink and rattle after she walks away.

Sam drums his finger tips on his knees. I look about. In this safe well-lit air conditioned room there is no one on guard. No one breaking squelch twice, whispering, "My sitreps are negative." No one to say, "Take five," or "Saddle up." There is no radio man shouting into the black plastic handset, "I say again! I say again!" No lieutenant shouting, "Move up, goddamn it! Move up!" No mortar crews firing harassing rounds. No casualties wailing, "Medic!! Medic!!"

There is a rattling noise. Mama-san shuffles in, a rum and Coke in each hand.

"You pay later," she says, through her painted smile.

The moment we reach for the icy drinks two young women in short skirts and thigh black boots enter the room and sit between us.

Sam turns toward me. "May I borrow your camera?" he asks. "I want to see Tokyo."

The whore seated next to him makes a hurtful face. "GI, no like?" she asks.

Sam presses his lips in perfect apology, takes the camera, waves good bye.

Her name is Yukio. We sit on the hard square bed in one of the small square rooms, surrounded by the simple decor of soap, towel, sink. She is slender, with an ivory face framed by jet black hair. Her bright red lips edge a delicate mouth of crowded white teeth. Her flimsy sweater contains inviting curves which make me hard. But I have fear. I have killed and cared for so many men but I've never slept with a woman.

"Can you help me?" I ask her. I pantomime holding my

rifle. "*Bang! Bang!* You understand?"

My whore nods without mercy.

After the ritual of money, after the time to undress, after she pulls me inside her, mechanically rotates her slim ivory hips, she grinds my virginity.

"Me goo fuck, GI," she says, yawning. "Me goo fuck."

The next day I take taxis driven by white gloved drivers, play Pachinko and pinball in noisy arcades, get lost in the subway system, escape from a horde of giggling school girls. In a vast teeming mall, an army of manikins in a riot of clothes strut and scream, "Buy me! Buy me!"

Another night, another whore. I can't wait to get back to Vietnam.

On the return flight, Sam shows me the photos he's taken: the city's immaculate green parks; an ancient stone temple nearly untouched by time; colossal skyscrapers; a museum dedicated to the delicate art of painted silk.

"I'm glad you had a good time," I say.

When Sam asks how things went I lie with all my heart.

In Phuc Vinh, the new lieutenant welcomes me to my new home. "I don't know about the bush," he says, "but back here you *will* salute officers. You *will* get haircuts. You *will* polish your boots."

Is he out of his mind? I can't do that. *I can't.* A month later I ask to be sent to LZ Green, a remote firebase near the Cambodian border.

"Fine with me, soldier," says the lieutenant.

Screw him. At least I'm out of the bush.

Each morning I drag a full barrel of shit out from beneath a mortar box shitter, pour diesel fuel into the stinking sludge, toss in a trip flare, over the hours, with a long metal stake, stir the burning muck to a fine white ash. At dusk I drag the barrel back, exchange it for new one brimming with shit.

Each day, the gun crews whisper, "How can he do that?" Screw them. Who cares what they think? During monsoon burning shit keeps you warm. Keeps you safe. Time passes quickly. I've got three weeks left in Vietnam. Twenty-one and a wake up, you understand?

A soldier yells, "Fire mission!" and immediately, the Howitzer crews aim and adjust their cannons, swiftly lift, push, ram the heavy shells home, insert powder bags, slap the hammers at the back of the breech. The cannons buck and roar, the silver shells arc into the clear blue sky, fade and disappear, then far away, a rumbling *boooom*.

The first sergeant is a tall thin man who has made a career of the army. "Lifers," we call them. Some have seen combat but most have not.

"Bravo company got ambushed," he says. "They lost a medic. The lieutenant says you got to go out. I'll pull you back in three days."

Is he out of his fucking mind? This is not my company. These are not my men. Fuck Bravo. Fuck them all. The days of my life are etched on a cardboard square kept inside a waterproof wallet, each day one step closer to home. Eight months on patrol. Half my platoon wounded or wasted. Twenty-one and a wake up, you understand?

"No way, Sarge. Fuck the lieutenant. No fucking way."

"That's a direct order," he shouts.

I gather my gear, walk to the chopper pad, watch the morning mist rise off the tarmac.

There are four new medics back in Phuc Vinh. Why isn't the lieutenant sending one of them to Bravo? Why me? Twenty-one days until I go home. I'm locked and loaded and melting down.

When the chopper swoops in the door gunner yells, "Get on! Get on!" but I shake my head 'no.' The pilot shakes a fist, yells at me, but the roar of the engines drown him out. He pulls pitch, lifts up and away. Ten minutes later a second Huey arrives.

"You going to Phuc Vinh?" I shout.

The gunner signals thumbs up. I clamber aboard.

After the short flight I jump out and begin the one klick trudge to the company aid station. My pack is heavy with C-rations, medical supplies, a half dozen one quart canteens. My .45 sits snug in its beat-up leather holster, tied round my leg with a bit of cord taken from a dead VC. Four frags are hooked to my pistol belt. Three bandoliers slap my chest with every step.

Soon my uniform clings to my skin, sweat pours down my face. At a bend in the road I spit at the mangy strays that tag behind me. I'm locked and loaded and melting down.

From fifty meters I spot the new lieutenant just as he exits the aid station. He is a handsome, clean shaven man, wearing a clean uniform and polished black boots. He is finishing up a smile but stops mid-stride at the sight of me.

As I walk toward him there is the slight crunching sound of my boots on the dry brittle earth. Water sloshes inside the plastic canteens. The full Bandoliers tap rhythmically against my chest. On its own my rifle levels itself at the lieutenant.

From twenty meters I hear a strange voice shouting, "Are you sending me out, motherfucker? Are you sending me out?"

The officer does not move. Does not speak. Slowly, he raises both hands over his head.

"I'm sorry," he mutters, and continues to tremble. "I'll send someone else."

I take one step back, lower my weapon, push the safety on, walk past the no-good-rat-fuck-rear-echelon-mother fucker, enter the aid station, push past the astonished new medic who will take my place, find his bunk, throw down my gear, and weep.

Years later, in a barren dusty field, I tell Mike Wilson, the platoon RTO, about meeting the new lieutenant. He listens intently, not once interrupting while I speak, then twice kicks at clumps of dirt.

"Jesus Christ, Doc," he says, as the dry earth explodes in

small white puffs. "I bet he thought you was gonna blow him away!"

"You know what, Michael? I never thought of that."

He knew exactly what I meant.

After Reaching The Home Of Juan Pablo Lorenz

In 1992 I bought a one way ticket to Guatemala. The goal: to learn Spanish, then return to New York to work with immigrants affected by brutal civil war and its aftermath. I spent my first month in the sleepy highland village of Todos Santos, and then I made a series of treks through Central America over the next eight months. Yet after each journey– El Salvador, Honduras, Mexico–I came back to dirt-poor, stunningly beautiful, unspoiled Todos Santos.

Saddled between the tall peaks of the Cuchumatanes, the town had two paved roads and three cars; flea-bitten dogs sunned themselves on the cobblestone streets. There were no phones, no banks, no televisions. Indoor plumbing was scarce. Hole in the wall *tiendas* – store fronts made artful by sun and rain sold snacks, bread, soda, candles, and purified water in clear plastic bags. Quetzelteca, said to keep the indigenous drunk and thereby quiet, cost twenty cents per pint.

In Todos Santos, the proud indigenous men wear straw hats, hand-loomed red and white striped trousers and white shirts with large embroidered collars. The strong but obedient women wear the customary ankle-length dark skirt and colorful hand-woven vests. At the time, most lived in dirt-floored, sparsely furnished adobe huts heated by wood burning stoves.

In the '80s, during Guatemala's Civil War, the village

was massacred twice. The Army used the church as a prison, cut off peasants' ears, set fire to feet, slaughtered mules, burnt crops, smashed tools, raped women. Such things occurred throughout Guatemala for quite some time.

"Vida es triste," say the peasants of Todos Santos. Life is sad. Most gringos haven't a clue about the arduous farm work, the cold nights, the search for wood to light the stoves, the sun-beaten crosses in the quiet green field two hundred meters past the town market, a monument to the town's tormented dead.

I lived two trails above town in a half-constructed cement house being built by thin, industrious Desidero and his plump wife Clementina. On the first floor was a dusty jumble of tools, electrical wires, and broken concrete blocks, but the cast cement stairwell led to my perfectly square room with a box spring bed and a naked light bulb that hung precariously from the ceiling by exposed red wires. On the south wall, an arched window overlooked a valley of emerald cornfields and steep mountains dotted with scrub and pine. At dawn, as excited roosters crowed, as waking women re-lit ashen fires, a wispy white fog descended from the mountains into the valley. My rent was ten dollars a month.

James, another gringo who occupied the room next door, slept in a Mexican hammock. Muscular and friendly, a frequent visitor who spoke impeccable Spanish, James earned the townspeople's trust.

Each morning, after a cold shower, after washing our clothes in the chipped cement sink by the chicken coop, after ringing out the wet cloth the Maya way, firmly twisting the water out inch by inch, hanging the laundry on a line atop the windswept roof, we walked the trail to Tres Olgitas, a dollar-a-night fire-trap of unheated rooms; the exquisite meals cooked by three young women always cheap and delicious.

Sometimes without James, I hiked the long steep mountain paths. Trekked them for hours. What compelled these wanderings I did not know.

"Where are you going?" asked the wheat-skinned villagers in their slow melodic Spanish. Their first language, M'am, so sharp and different with its frequent glottal stops.

"For a walk," I answered, beginning the long ascent.

Each day they ask, "Why, mister? Why do you walk?"

"For the exercise," I say.

Dumbfounded, they smile. Only fools work without compelling reason.

Another war—one with a prickly tangle of jungle and vines, its stifling green curtain of infinite heat, a war in Asia where sudden shots made dry red dirt more crimson than war, with its walking dead and ancestral spirits—dogged my every step. I did not know it.

Once, when trucks from far-off cities and towns arrived with bales of used clothing, when distant villagers came to sell house wares, farms tools, meat from hanging carcasses, aromatic spices in wicker baskets or burlap sacks, an array of fresh vegetables, I wept before walking. It happened like this: Tugging on my jeans, buttoning my red cotton shirt, lacing up my leather boots; somewhere in town a man or boy struck a match to a string of firecrackers which announced Market Day. But this time I heard the crackle of AK-47s and M-16s, felt the heated downdraft from chopper blades, shook and sobbed until the flashback in a town twice massacred, in a country that had seen decades of devils, vanished.

Like a good lieutenant, James does not get lost. When the sun fails to burn away the mists of impenetrable white, he marches forward, deftly twirling a hand-carved Kendo stick, as if chopping the clouds in half.

Past the easy main trail, past the ladder-like gauntlet of switchbacks that force us to crawl or constrict or stretch our bodies, we climb to eleven thousand feet. On a grassy spot we slip off our packs, sit and gulp purified water. After a time, two peasant boys dressed in colorful rags drew near like jackals. I reach into my shirt pocket.

"Here, I give this to you," I say, in Spanish.

A few cigar puffs later the boys cough and giggle and set the grass on fire. We help them extinguish the blaze, say to them *"Adios,"* then trek the last thousand meters to the home of Juan Pablo Lorenz.

We've never asked Juan Pablo why he lives at the mountaintop. Why he has chosen this lonely life. The Altiplano, unlike the fertile valley, is a landscape of desolate but spectacular outcroppings and skeletal trees, which stand out against the clear sky, the receding ranks of the pastel Cuchumatanes. Here, at twelve thousand feet, the thin air imparts a supernatural feel to all sight and sound. A crow's wings claps like thunder. The bark of a dog is a frightful event.

"Bienvenidos," says Juan Pablo, shooing away the excited pet. *"Pasen adelante... pasen..."*

Few people visit here, but nearly all villagers have dogs to warn of thieves. Stepping forward, we crouch to enter the low doorway of the large hut built from timber planks stood on end. Juan Pablo, perhaps in his twenties, is a thin, happy man with a broad handsome face; a half moon smile reveals his large white teeth; his thick black hair pokes out from a traditional straw woven hat. His pretty young wife, Elizabeta, carries their frightened infant daughter on her back in vibrant cloth stitched with ancient Maya patterns. "Mmm... mmm..." she hums to her child. But still it whimpers.

In the center of the dirt floor, James, Juan Pablo and I sit around a three-stone fire place. Behind us, in the dim light that peeks through the cracks between the upright boards, a kitten prowls through shards of broken pottery, dried chicken bones, wood shavings, newspapers, cardboard boxes. Here, an hour's walk from town, nothing is thrown out. Juan Pablo leans forward, turns his head sideways, and gently blows on the embers until the wood crackles and bursts into flame. The wood planks reflect our shivering shadows.

The rising smoke exits through a small blackened hole in

the roof. The fire slowly draws the chill from us. I offer gifts: bread, hard-baked cooking chocolate purchased in Antigua, a pound of unshelled peanuts, four tins of milk, a large felt blanket.

"Gracias." says Juan Pablo, but then asks, *"Por qué?"*

I don't know why I climb so hard each day or if I need to help this man survive.

Elizabeta begins the ritual of making tortillas. She has already ground the corn in the traditional manner, whetted it into a thick white paste. In the warm hut, as her body shifts to the patter of her moistened palms, which quietly slap and press the dough into patties, the anxious child is lulled to sleep. One by one Elizabeta sets the bread disks onto a circular pan she has placed over the fire. One by one she turns the tortillas over with her finger tips. In these moments of tapping palms, the padded step of the playful cat, the burning wood sliding into itself, in this land of Maya dressed in brilliant patterns, of clandestine graves and unbridled beauty, James is puzzled by my tears but does not ask why I cry. And if he did I would not be able to tell him.

We say *"Adios"* to Juan Pablo. Goodbye to his wife, to the sleeping child, the slumbering kitten, the vigilant dog.

The return trek goes well. Like the Maya on steep trails, we tilt our bodies back, taking short hurried steps as we trot downhill. On the main wide trail, we run in curves which absorb our momentum so we do not to trip or fall or tumble over the mountain. We arrive at the village in half the time it took to reach the home of Juan Pablo Lorenz.

I say goodbye to James. "See you tomorrow," he says. Then he is off for a communal meal at Tres Olgitas.

There are no customers yet at Comedor Katy's, a restaurant of two cement rooms furnished with simple pine tables and chairs; there are no menus, there is no music. An indigenous girl takes my order. It is always the same: a large bowl of vegetable soup, a plate of rice and chicken.

"Sopa de verduras," she always asks. "Y pollo?"

"Si," I say. "Y pollo."

The girl leaves. In the dirt yard out back there is the sound of flapping wings, scampering feet, desperate squawks and final cackles. A cut to the neck and the bird is dead.

Waiting for the meal to cook, I see a small boy peering through the half open door; I wave to him. Barefoot, he wears torn dirty clothes, a hat with a hole in it, his face a mixture of hope and fear. He stares at me. I know this child; he has often approached then run away whenever I've climbed or descended the mountain alone. I make a welcoming gesture. The boy hesitates, then runs in and sits in the chair opposite me.

"What would you like?" I ask.

"Naranja," he says, pointing to an empty bottle on a nearby table.

I call to a young woman in the kitchen lording over large kettles atop a wood burning stove. *"Señorita,"* I say.

She steps out from behind a curtain, her face and hands moist and pink.

"Uno, por mi amigo," I say, pointing.

The girl nods; disappears, moment later sets a new bottle on the table. The boy, perhaps eight years old, cannot contain his excitement. I pry the metal cap off with the tip of a knife. He grasps the bottle with both hands, lifts it to his mouth, and guzzles the thick orange drink. Nothing I can do will change his plight but for now he is happy.

Tacked to the far wall is a colorful poster of gringo Jesus, his arms held wide open, palms turned upward, as if to embrace the world. His parted shirt reveals a split open chest; bolts of yellow light streak from his red sacred heart. As the boy drinks the sugar water, as King Jesus holds his sacred smile, as the soft clink of silverware is not the biting song of bullets, the girl sets the bowl of simmering vegetables, the plate of meat and rice, on the table. The aromatic steam fills the room. The boy stares at the feast but is silent. There is much hunger in proud Todos Santos.

"Pollo, por mi amigo," I say to the girl.

Suddenly a middle-aged woman steps out from behind the curtain, with all her might hurls her sandal at a skeletal dog, drawn by the scent of food. She yells at the gaunt creature. A hundred glottal curses fill the air.

My legs and body tremble. The boy looks at me strange.

"Que pasa, señor?" he asks. *"Tiene fria? Por qué se agita? Por qué?"*

What's happening, little friend? No, it's not the cold mountain air or shivery chills but the sight of the thrown sandal and the sound of your last words that whisk me back in time.

Enemy grenades, primitive but effective, more often maimed Americans than killed them. During the ambush, after the snap of the chemical fuse, caused by pulling a bit of string, the invisible enemy hurled the wood handled grenade at us. It fell short but the blast twisted the machine gun's barrel as if it were clay. Someone threw one of ours, a smooth nasty little bomb with a killing range of five meters. After the fiery blast a sergeant thought we'd killed them all. But then a second snap, and this time the grenade landed between us and we five soldiers scampered away but not soon enough. *BOOM!* And we lay screaming.

But what can I say to you, my friend, that your family or neighbors do not know? What could I say, and how could I say it and what difference would it make in your world?

The dog yelps and scampers away. The angry woman picks up her shoe. The boy upends the bottle and drains it dry.

"Gracias, amigo," he says, smacking his orange stained lips. *"Gracias."* Then he is gone.

That night–after walking the small trails to Desidero's house, trudging up the cement stair case, after turning off the naked light bulb and laying down in my box spring bed in my square room overlooking the fertile valley, cloaked by darkness, sheltered beneath a felt blanket, before sleep overtook me–my tears fell like rain.

Bluefields

MK would have stopped me with a tap to the chest. Made a joke of it all. He would have laughed.

It is a two-hour ride up the Rio Escondido in the canoe-like fiberglass boat fitted with high-power outboard engines. The panga's curved bow frequently lifts up, slaps the turbulent water; a cold white mist sprays up; the sleek boat speeds forward, slows down, zigzags the switch-back channels, zooms ahead. By noon we five peace activists reach the town–devastated by the merciless gales of the hurricane. We disembark, careful not to tip the craft–to fall into the murky poison–single file cross a narrow wood bridge that leads to shore. Beneath us, as if dreaming, a dead dog rhythmically bobs in the maculate water, as if this were a welcoming gesture. The others turn their heads away, but I am fascinated by the obscene lullaby, the melody of death by drowning. Captivated.

We activists have come to visit local villagers, the town mayor, a women's group, a farm collective, a human rights worker. But until our bodies adjust to the heat, we will half-doze as they discuss their concerns, successes, grievances. Even the celebrated Rubin Hamilcar, political leader, and survivor of three assassination attempts by the American-backed guerrillas ("Contras" as they are known), cannot undo our lethargy.

It is 1990, the thirteen-year conflict has recently ended, yet hangs like a dark sky over the ruined tropic land. The violent scent of suffering and loss, the stench of storm debris, the aromatic rot of all things organic, infiltrates everything. Still, it is impossible not to feel, hear, taste, Nicaragua's electric tension. It resides in the people, the country, in the swollen ground beneath our feet.

Out of common interests, the two women, the priest, the builder, and I have banded together, flown from Miami to Managua, bussed, trucked, walked, hitched to villages where the Sandinista revolution played itself out.

"Yes, Father, yes," the two women sometimes say when Father Allen talks. Like the other man in the group, whose name is William, I too am most often quiet. When Margaret asked, "What about you, Robert? What do you do? What brings you here?" I did not hesitate to tell the old lie, to put on the pleasing mask that hides my pain like sterile white gauze over a deep puncture wound. "I'm married," I said. "Two kids. Wife works. I'm a stay-at-home-dad. Like to travel. Take pictures. Want to learn more about Central America. Got the chance, so here I am." At the moment she smiled, my heart went cold.

On the outskirts of Leon sits an abandoned, weed-infested, roofless jail. Upon entering, the first thing one sees is the execution site. At two-meter intervals, a cement wall is pitted with heart-high bullet holes. Here, blindfolded prisoners stood mute, shots rang out, bodies crumpled into pools of red. Further on, inside dank unlocked cells, iron-bar gates hang from their hinges, tendrils of rusting concertina wire curl like bougainvillea over the crumbled brick walls. Here and there, graffiti bloom on rotted plaster, like dried flowers.

In this town, in many towns, shackled men were tossed down wells; women and children were shot by Contras. Today the dark-skinned, proud-faced surviving villagers welcome us.

"*Bienvenidos,*" they say. "*Bienvenidos,*" because we gringos will buy handicrafts and souvenirs. Our gringo money will buy precious food, clothes, tools, infant's milk, help families take back their lives. That is how it works. Life goes on, no matter what the outcome of revolution.

By foot, by truck, and now by panga we have shared a bit of ourselves as we travel to reach the twice-devastated, aptly named Bluefields, whose feisty people refuse not to resist—because that too would mean death.

On our first night, after settling into a fire-trap shanty of a guest house, lit at the whim of thrumming diesel generators, where the door locks are broken, the ceiling fans inoperable, the torn window screens beyond repair, a young boy, driven by hunger tries to steal my wallet and valuables during a blackout. In the darkness, his phantom hand parts the screen, walks the rickety table-top like a flesh-toned tarantula; his calculating fingertips one-by-one probing for wealth. Invisible, I strike him hard in the face and he flees into the night never to return. Poor bastard. I should have cut his arm off. But my machete, taken from a dead man killed in a distant war, lies deep in the depths of my catacomb mind. *Buried*, I tell you. *Buried*.

Father Allen is a middle-aged Catholic priest. He sports a well kempt beard, is curly headed, somewhat portly, and wears wire-rim spectacles which obscure the circles beneath his eyes. A concerned expression imbues his face, yet he is always affable. He is overly friendly, yet sincere. This paradox has a pleasing effect. Wearing blue jeans, a white T-shirt and hiking shoes like the rest of us, he leads our morning meal with a prayer. "Our Father," he begins. His thumb and index finger pinch and pass his rosary beads in their infinite cycle. His eyes close as he recites the verse by heart.

Standing around the table, Ann, a medical student, whose shyness increases her beauty, and Margaret, a plump, gentle, gray-haired woman and self-employed graphic designer, mouth Father Allen's sacerdotal chant. Standing near them at the foot of the guest-house breakfast table is William. A stocky balding man, a home contractor by trade, his large open face is anchored by a boxer's pug nose, framed by large flat ears. William, who is six-feet tall and forty-six years old, takes an aspirin a day for the health of his heart. He misses his wife. On the trip up river, he confided to me her last words, but his voice was drowned out by the engines' dull roar.

As Father Allen prays, my mind goes blank. *It has nothing to do with the battalion Chaplin's funereal chant, the rockets' surprise white-tailed WHOOSH, the orange flash, the crew cut head borne aloft in a crimson halo of brain and bone. It has nothing to do with Vietnam.* Better to contemplate the breakfast laid out on the black-and-white, checkered table cloth: thick creamy yoghurt, large wood trays of pineapple, bananas, melon, loaves of warm fresh bread, brightly colored glasses of steaming hot coffee, ice-cold juice. When we are done, it is time for our ration of Bluefields. We peaceful gringos will hike from this town of two thousand people to a destroyed settlement an hour away.

Father Allen walks first. Ann pairs up with Margaret. William and I walk behind. As we stroll past the outskirts of town, picking our way through piles of rubble, Margaret makes small talk. Ann says she's never been to a third-world country. In fact, she has never traveled outside the United States. She is studying to be a surgeon. She wants to help people who need medical aid. Reaching back, she slips an elastic band over her silky brown hair to make a pony tail. Margaret thinks that is a wonderful idea, helping people.

Past a bend in the road, Margaret points to a ruined, open-air market whose wood stalls are bent, broken and lacquered in the recent hurricane's earthy muck and sickening slime. Somewhere on this trip, she hopes to purchase a half-bolt of embroidered cloth she has seen elsewhere. She will mount it across her living room wall. This will help promote dialog between her dinner guests, she says. Ann, who has clear insouciant eyes, rosy cheeks, an aquiline nose perched atop soft red lips, says all the colors in this world are beautiful.

"Beautiful," she says.

William whispers that we are old enough to be Ann's father. There's no need to say we are taken by her beauty. I do not tell William that once I had many women like her. Affairs. Flings. One night stands. Then, like heartless clockwork, all the pretty girls were cast off like ruined clothes, worn out shoes, equipment no longer needed. A dozen times I tell myself I must be kind to her. Must do that. Be kind.

William talks about his dead wife, how much he loved her, cared for her, misses her. When he goes silent, I chat with Margaret and Ann. We are all chatting and talking as Father Allen leads us past the beautiful wreckage of Bluefields.

After ninety minutes of brisk walking, we reach our destination. There is not much left of the village. Everything has been washed away, pried apart, scavenged, or stolen. The land itself is riven by water. It is bleak. Despoiled. Barren. Feverishly, those survivors who can build new homes made of sturdy, cast cement. The less fortunate jury-rig scraps of wood, plastic sheeting, and cardboard boxes to make lean to's or skeletal shelters. There is the sharp crack of hammers hitting the tops of flat-head nails. There is the archeology of hoisting up and setting-to- place the heavy, white slabs. Chickens scratch and peck the bare earth in hopes of food.

We come upon a wrinkle-faced woman who sits glassy-eyed in a threadbare hammock strung between two metal stakes. Scattered around her like rose petals, a circle of crumpled rags are all that remain of her world. As the old woman rocks herself in shocked-out lullaby, Ann breaks down in a torrent of tears. We are all deeply touched; but Father Allen, William, and Margaret—whatever their principles, whatever their motives—cannot bring themselves to comfort Ann. Really comfort her. No. The priest, the widower, the elder woman can only muster words of advice. Words. Without thinking, I sweep Ann into my arms and hold her. Hold her close. Until she is quieted and calm. While the others gape and the glassy-eyed woman sways further into oblivion, I cup the crescent of Ann's ear and whisper, "It's all right. The people will help her. That's the way it works. OK?" Ann whimpers, nestles her yearning face into the crook of my neck. This makes me uncomfortable.

In my best loving, take-charge voice, I say, "Ann, there's nothing we can do. She'll be alright."

I have comforted many men in extreme distress. Lied to them, flat out lied with all my heart. Gave them hope, courage, stabbed them with morphine until the choppers drew near and flew them away along with pieces of my heart. My lying heart.

We trespassers say goodbye to the dazed woman, good-bye to the villagers, continue taking in third-world sights. We pass a sky-blue, wood shack, raised on stilts, that has somehow survived the storm. Beneath it, four pigs lay half submerged in a pool of filth and mud. The shack has no windows. Only a single plywood door, opened to let out the stifling heat. Inside, a toddler, dressed in rags, sits in front of a blank TV set. She waves at us. She smiles. Then returns to waiting for images that will take her away. The mud-caked pigs lift their heads, blink, and squeal as we walk past.

We laugh, but we are not laughing. On the way back to town, William and I walk first, the women are behind us. Father Allen follows.

To pass the time, to avoid his comments about helping Ann, I tell William about MK, the best joke teller in the world. I tell William that MK's jokes are the most obscene jokes I have ever heard. I describe MK's perfect pace, impeccable diction, unbeatable timing. I describe the art of setting the stage, the semantic science of compelling cross-purposes, the psychology of paradox. I tell William how MK ropes his listeners with silken wit, slips the invisible noose around their necks, tightens the penultimate lines, then jerks the loop shut. I tell William that MK has caused grown men to rock—livid with laughter—slap their knees, pound their thighs, stomp the floor. I tell William that MK never fails to burst wide the sacred ancestral gates that each of us secretly wants to breach.

When I'm done speaking, William, whose dour mood has ticked up, takes the hint, tells me a joke. It is good, it is tame, it is appropriate. Something his dead wife would have approved. At the predictable punch line, we laugh good hearted-laughter and pat each other's backs. It's good to see William happy. *Maybe tomorrow I will tell him that, at the final gut-bursting line, MK, who always leads the riotous cheers, roars loudest of all, howls great gales, turns bright red, and no one, not one person, has ever suspected that his depraved, vile humor serves a secret purpose. No one suspects MK's hidden life.*

Margaret and Ann, who are thirty yards ahead, stop to look back.

"What's so funny?" asks Margaret. She looks at me in a curious way. Ann dips her head as if she were in thought.

Like adolescents, William and I have been caught-out playing a school yard prank.

Williams says, "Nothing."

I say, "Nothing." We pretend atonement. We pantomime shame.

Margaret smirks, as if she has uncovered an inner truth. Like a schoolmarm, she knits her brows, wags her index finger at us, whispers to Ann, who feigns agreement.

Father Allen, who trails behind us by twenty yards, says, "Keep moving. We should keep moving."

After forty-five minutes, we are not far from town. At a muddy crossroads, I stop, reach into my day-pack, fish out my camera. The others wait as I prepare to take the photograph. Two young boys struggle to drag a bull's head across the washed-out street. They breathe hard, they grunt, push, tug the sharp horns, trudge forward. The animal's large, glutinous, unblinking eyes, the water-color trail of gore and innards, the cloud of swarming insects, the boys singing with laughter: *Such moments are like the shadows which run across the tall grass and lose themselves in sunset. Or the shrill whistle of steam rising from a boiling kettle in an empty kitchen.* As the lilt of their joy carries on the hot tongue of a tropical breeze, I take the picture, take it, take it, click, click, click. Then the cheerful boys and the monster are gone but they have taken me back in time.

There are seventeen of us. MK walks point. We step, sway, crawl through the jungle, like snakes on water. The hoot of monkeys, the cackle of birds, these things hide our movement. At exactly the right time and place, we form a perimeter. We wait, watch, listen. At exactly the right time, we move forward, undetected, pay out our intersecting trip-wire, stake the flares, stake the intersecting mines. Retreat. Spaced five meters apart in a tight circle, we sleep with the detonators on our chests. We sleep with knives, machetes, grenades, with our weapons locked and loaded. We take two-hour shifts on guard. No one knows we are here. In the morning, ten men fan out in the four compass directions. They crouch low, step quiet, unclip the wires, deactivate the mines, slink back to cover. When the enemy strikes, a curtain of steel rakes over us and fifteen Rangers are wounded or dead. In the scream-lit chaos, the enemy charge. We growl like wolves. We snarl like dogs. We are fighting hand to hand. MK is shot. I am shot. MK is bayoneted but kills the girl with his forty-five. Mutilates her. Then we run.

From that time, we have never talked about it. I take pills, talk to doctors, travel to parts of the world where war has left its anguished print. MK drinks hard. Works hard. Laughs hard. These are the ways we choose to survive.

On our fourth day our good-will party rises early to trek two miles to Finca Libertad. The directions we have are quite simple. "Take the washed-out road, follow the curves east, then north, for one hour," a thin old man, wearing torn pants, threadbare sneakers, his palm outstretched, tells us. Margaret, who speaks Spanish well, translates. "Don't worry," he says. "Let the road lead you." Without a word, each of us digs into our pockets and gives him money. Making our way out of town, we listen to the retreating waves, the cackle of multi-hued macaws, chattering squadrons of soaring green parrots, the fall of our footsteps on the dark dense earth.

The farm is gone. Nothing is left of the corn but the faint imprint of long, furrowed lanes, piles of dead leaves, withered stalks. A large campesino family gathers round us. The men, women, and children, have been working since sun-up. Margaret engages a stalwart young man who has a double-faced ax that rests on his shoulder. Within seconds, a broad smile sweeps across the angular features of his caramel face.

"Yes, yes. We would like you to help us with our work," he says. "We would like that very much."

The excited children draw near, inspect our well-made clothes, tap our clear-plastic canteens, press their fingertips to our nylon daypacks, admire our handsome, speed-lace, trekking boots. The dark-eyed women make secret talk by shielding their mouths with the flat of their hands. The sturdy men give us tools, assign us tasks. It is that simple. For the next five hours, we gringos take part in the work of reclaiming the land. Teams of men trim, chop and lasso logs, haul them away. The women and children collect stones, branches, roots, toss them in wicker baskets they haul on their backs. The sooner the land is cleared, the sooner it dries, the sooner it will be furrowed and replanted. That is the goal of the hardworking *collectivistas*. That is what they want: to bring the farm back to life.

As the sun rises overhead, we gringos cannot keep up

with the arduous pace. We stoop, stretch, guzzle long gulps from our clear canteens which are filled with purified water. We stop to wipe the sweat and crud from our eyes, but continue to work. Over the back-breaking hours, few words are spoken, but much is said and done by a nod here, a glance there. That is what counts: to work with the campesinos who have lost everything to weather and war; to help.

At precisely four o'clock, a young girl motions us to set down our tools. Hungry and tired, we are led to a large, round, plank table ringed by dozens of hand-made chairs. With the men, women, and children, we sit and partake in the simple meal accompanied by the textured sounds of coarse bread being broken in half; the scraping of wooden spoons inside bowls; by children smacking their lips as they savor the last scraps of burnt-black meat. When it is time to go, many hands pat our arms. Many voices give thanks. On the road back, Father Allen, Margaret, William and Ann step lively as they talk and talk. *I have known this perfect paradox – feeling most alive when most exhausted, but our eyes told more than we could ever tell of what we did or what was done to us.* For some reason, the others take no notice that I'm quiet. Later, I have trouble sleeping. The next day, to celebrate, we go up-river.

It is a one-hour panga ride to El Bluff, a remote hamlet spared the furious brunt of the storm. The long, pristine white beach is deserted. Stands of tall palm trees encircle the blue waters which lap at the shoreline. We will spend a few hours here, return to Bluefields by dusk. As we disembark, the short wiry boatman, whom we have paid in advance, points to a half- hidden thatched hut at the top of a forested ridge. There are horses to rent, he says. Then he tugs the bill of his yellow, baseball cap, and guns the engines; the twin motors spit clouds of blue smoke, and–with a great roaring sound–the prow lifts, the boat jets forward–a trail of fizzing white foam in its wake.

We are wearing bathing suits beneath our clothes.

Margaret and Ann, Father Allen and William, jog straight to the beach, undress, wade out into the sweet sting of the water.

"Robert," cries Ann. The shimmering blue ocean clings to her hips as she turns around. "Robert, where are you going?"

I have not yet shaken off yesterday's language of semaphore. Raising my left hand, I point to the emerald ridge, the simple hut, the distant horizon. For a split second our eyes lock. Does she see it? Then, dimples appear on either side of her face. Ann raises both arms over her head, turns back, plunges dolphin-like into the sea.

There is no need to knock. There is no door. Two layers of tattered netting are tacked to the entrance frame. When no one answers I push the netting aside. In the center of the dirt-floor room there is a three-stone fireplace. The embers beneath a blackened kettle have gone out. On the far wall, a book-sized mirror hangs above an old, wood table. There is the scent of soot and the passing of time. Sunlight illuminates the floating dust that fills the air.

Footsteps. A man. As I turn to face him, his husky voice says, "You are the one who came up the hill. You are here for the horses, yes?" A tall, muscular, swarthy man, with bronzed skin, dark eyes, shoulder-length hair, he extends his calloused, right hand to me.

"I am Marcelino Ramirez," he says. As if he were a bridge connecting one moment to the next. As if he can see, feel, hear many things all at the same time. As if his real work in this life is to keep himself whole. I stare at the maverick patchwork of welts and scars that spangle the right side of his neck.

"From the Contras," he says, without blinking.

Marcelino shapes his hand pistol-like, pulls the trigger twice. I know the phrase to express sorrow, so I say it. "Lo siento, Señor. Lo siento." *I do know.*

Marcelino does not reply. Instead, after touching palms, we leave the hut; walk a short distance to a half-acre clearing.

A mare and two stallions swish their tails, lift their ears, sway their heads toward us. Marcelino makes a clicking noise by repeatedly pressing the tip of his tongue to the roof of his mouth, retracting it back. The big, tan horses amble up to him like obliging children.

"This one," I say, running my hands over the mane of the mare. "I'll take this one."

There are no stirrups. There is no saddle. Only a white plastic rope, fitted for reins, which Marcelino uncoils from his pants pocket.

"Gingi," he says, calming the horse as he slides the rope over her head.

At the sound of her name Gingi pokes at the earth with her right hoof.

I point to the beach. Pantomime riding.

"OK," says Marcelino. "One hour, one American dollar." Walking away, he points to the hut. "On the table," he says. Then he is gone.

In the dream, I'm standing knee-deep in the ocean with a large black horse. The water is clear and cool. Overhead, the ribs of sun-tipped clouds fill the blue sky. I put my arms around the horse's neck. "I love you," I say. The animal flares its nostrils. Snorts, shimmies, lowers its neck and head. Nuzzles me. When I step back, it gallops away. Love. For one solid hour, I lay still, saturated by the rapture of this perfect word.

I canter Gingi over long stretches of glistening beach. Wheel her about, dig my heels into her heaving flanks. I crouch, lean forward, growl her name, growl it into her raised ears as her galloping hooves kick up sand and foaming surf. Six times we climb the steep hill, six times we descend. On the last trip up, I dismount. The moment I release the white harness, the exhausted horse bolts, takes her place among the stallions, who whinny, ripple their necks, draw near and console her with the sides of their muzzles.

"Gingi...Gingi..." But there is no answer.

I leave money in the hut. Walk to the far end of the shoreline. For an hour, listen to the murmuring waves roll and retreat. Then walk to where the others have gathered. The boat will arrive soon. The blood red sun touches the tip of the sea. There is tension here. I can feel it the closer I approach.

Margaret sits cross-legged, like a monk in contemplation. At the sound of my footsteps, she straightens her back, opens her eyes.

"We watched you riding," she says. Her question does not disguise her concern. "Where did you learn to do that?"

I kneel on the sand next to her. "Do what?" I ask.

They have been talking amongst themselves. Why don't they just say it?

"You didn't just ride," says William. He scowls, raises one hand, points to the hill. "You raced that horse. You punished it. You never let it rest."

"Something's bothering you," says Ann. Standing up, her brown hair falls to her shoulders in ringlets. "I noticed it the first day we met. Something...I don't know..." Her voice brims with feeling. "What is it, Robert? Tell me. Tell me what's wrong."

I want to tell them the beautiful dream of one year ago. I want to tell them it is not easy to live without love. Tell them my last love said late at night that I thrashed in her arms, called out names, made animal sounds, kicked and tossed, once gripped her neck so tightly she fought to wake me. I want to tell them the human voice can soar to inhuman heights when caught in the steely claws of modern or primitive weaponry. I want to tell them I have seen good men swiftly convert from sorrow to savagery like trusted grandfather clocks gone mad or merciful monks gone crazy. I want to...apologize.

I pretend to rub sand off my face so that William, Margaret, Father Allen, Ann, will not see what I am thinking. *I must apologize.*

Must do that.

I stand up. Hands flat at my sides I look to each of them: Margaret, her narrowed face a portrait of pain; Ann, lithe, generous, lenient; William, his furrowed widower's brow racked by discomfort. Father Allen begins to speak, but his words stop as the drone of the engines carries over the water. We scurry about, gather our things, hurry to the spot where the boat will meet us, sit quiet on the short ride back.

Our last day in Bluefields. The town mayor has arranged a clandestine meeting with Contras. The sound of their name brings fear. The ex-guerillas hate the locals, who given the chance, might kill them. First there was civil war. Then natural disaster. A cease fire has yielded uneasy calm.

The midday sun slants down on the single-story, concrete building, which has survived the storm intact. After we enter, the doors are locked by unseen hands. The windows are shuttered. In the dim light, we take seats that face a small stage. A fat man with sunglasses, a trim, straight-backed man, and a fierce-eyed boy sit on three legged stools like stone gods. All have their arms folded across their chests. All are grim faced. There is no translator. The Contras speak fluent English.

After brief, opening remarks, come the polite questions, shallow answers. No one dares to upset the balance. No one wants to create, or sound, an alarm. Nicaragua's uncivil tension is hiding, or is forcing itself to sleep.

"Where did you get your training?" asks Father Allen, breaking the silence.

"We're not allowed to say," says the black-haired, wheat-skinned boy, who wears green trousers, tan boots, a white T-shirt.

"What are your political beliefs?" asks Margaret.

"We are anti-communists," says the straight-backed man. He is well groomed, clean- shaven. "We fought subversive elements. We are freedom fighters," he says.

When asked, about religion, the Contra's bicker. The trim

man says they are good Catholics. They read the bible. They confess their sins. They have never done anything wrong.

Ann and Father Allen nod but Margaret raises up from her seat. She pats the hair at the base of her neck. An expectant look fills her face, seeps into her voice.

"Is it possible that innocent people were injured in Bluefields?" she asks.

The large man taps his foot, adjusts his glasses. The boy keeps still. The captain–for that is the rank stitched to his collar–lifts his right hand, holds it steady. Speaks.

"Our orders were never to shoot unarmed civilians," he says. "We never did that. We obeyed the law."

He's lying. Flat out lying. Why is he doing that? What's going on? There are bright lights, there are no lights, there is the sound of enemy gunfire, torrents of blood inside my head. There is the sound of no one breathing.

In the dream, we are overrun by enemy troops. I wake up, unholster my forty-five, point it at the feet of the man sleeping next to me. Pull the hammer back. The moon comes out from behind the clouds. I recognize the American boot-treads, don't fire, point the pistol straight up, pinch the hammer, pull the trigger, set the hammer into place, slip the weapon in my holster, go back to sleep. Never tell him.

An incandescent stream jets from the depths of my catacomb mouth:

"You bastards burnt down villes. Massacred people. Killed animals. Torched the fields. Murderers. You goddamn murderers. Why did you do it? Why?"

My locked-and-loaded, bandolier-laden, .45-caliber pistol, grenades-in-the-pistol belt, ice-in-the-veins, machete-wielding voice ricochets round and round in the sweltering room.

William, one seat away, reaches across, taps my shoulder. Margaret hisses cat-like. Even Ann makes a shushing noise. The three of them stare at me as if I'm a poisoned thing. A strange tormented voice curses each one of them. Finally I'm quiet.

The boy leans forward. Glares. "Mister," he says, "I never

killed anyone who did not need to be killed."

The heavy-set man intones, "I don't know where you get your facts, señor, but they are very wrong. We are freedom fighters. Didn't you hear? We fought for freedom." He smiles, pokes his dark glasses back up the bridge of his nose, waits for the storm to pass. For several seconds, no one speaks.

"Now that the war is over..." says Father Allen.

He pinches and pulls the triangular tip of his beard. He is a thoughtful man. *What are you thinking, Father Allen? What will you ask? Another polite question to avoid further conflict? A philosophical query that will lead nowhere? C'mon padre. Surprise me. Show me you have guts. Show me you know that the sinners of this world–the whores, junkies, cons, lowlifes, drunks, pimps, beggars, thieves, freaks, punks, fags, killers–show me you know that the scum of the earth who line the sewers of hell–show me you know they are your true brothers and sisters. Show me you know that. Show me, you son-of-a-bitch. Show me you got guts.*

Father Allen takes a deep breath.

"...What sort of work do you do and..."

In the time between speaking and not speaking, a puzzled look inhabits his middle-aged face. It's as if all the beliefs which sustain him, nourish him, protect him from all that is evil in this world and the next, have broken down.

"...Do you get along with the people who were once your enemy?" he asks.

This stray bullet digs straight into the open sore, the bright, festering wound, the peeled-back skin that refuses to heal in sad, resilient Nicaragua. The Contras are hated by their countrymen. But the boy and the corpulent man, following their Captain's secret cue, deny any hint of social discord, physical pain, emotional hardship. They have good jobs, they have good houses, they have wives and children, they have land, equipment, crops. They are happy. They are content. They have fought for freedom and freedom brings peace. They are peaceful freedom fighters. *Peace.*

The pause which follows is like the time between rumbling thunder and thunderous rain, the struggling moments between waking and dream-filled sleep, the calm before the hidden blast that erupts in a halo of perfect hell.

This is the time to set things right. No one anticipates my complete change of style, my transformed demeanor, my out-of-the-blue confession. Not Ann, not Margaret, not the builder or priest. Not even the terra-cotta, granite-faced Contras, who listen, while the knuckles of my hands, which grip the edge of my seat, turn white.

"Do you have nightmares?" I ask. "Do you jump or drop at sudden sounds? Do you think about killing people or that people want to kill you? Ever feel that you have no feelings? Ever feel like you don't belong? Do you get sad or lonely? Do you get depressed and drink too much? What about thoughts of killing yourself? What about anger? Shame? What about sorrow and guilt? Ever feel like the war is happening right now? "

The Contras shift about on their low set stools. The Captain, with new life in his eyes, draws breath, clears his throat, speaks to each of us. Like the dead dog, the bulls blood and the midnight thief, the unexpected is happening. In wind-torn, flooded-out, blown-down, phoenix-ash Bluefields...in a darkened room...a half dead man rises lotus-like from the depths of his tropical mud.

The Captain says that, after the fighting, he continued to live in the jungle, and each morning woke with blood in his mouth. "Blood in my mouth," he repeats. The Captain says the anger made him grab his weapon, lock it, load it, raise up, walk about, look for someone to kill. But the war is over, there is no one to shoot, he is going crazy. The Captain says, in the jungle, he found a bush doctor who mixed handfuls of long-stemmed herbs, a bush doctor who said: light these things, inhale the smoke, and you will be well. With his graceful hands, the Captain wafts invisible smoke into his squinting face. He inhales the fumes, holds his breath, exhales. After twenty minutes, he put the burning stalks down and slept three days straight. When he woke, he was cured.

"The blood, it is gone," the Captain says. "Gone."

The boy unfolds his arms to reveal the silk-screened words "Nantucket Rectilinear" stenciled across his shirt. He will not reveal his name. He tells us fireworks, firecrackers, backfiring cars, bright lights, cause him to crouch, run, hide. He reaches behind his back, lifts the tail of his shirt, delves, brandishes a snub-nosed thirty-eight. From where I sit, I can see the tips of the bullets chambered in the rotating-cylinder.

"I take her wherever I go," says the boy. "Wherever I go, I take her."

The women gasp, so he puts it away.

Boy, tell them more. Tell these innocent, caring gringos what it's like. Boy, tell them how you are never the same. Tell them all the rote drills, spirited hurrahs, drunken or silken hero talk, tell them it vanishes the instant the first fire fight, rocket or mortar attack, throws you down, shocks you out, barrels you into the split-second energetic world of hunting and being hunted by other human beings.

Boy, speak of the rattling bullets, speak of the white-tailed rockets, speak of ruby-tipped flesh and ripped torsos spangled with gore. Speak of that soft, dull thud on red-stained earth. Boy, speak of the last look in the dull eyes, the light gone out. Death. Speak of its feel, its smell, its touch. Speak of the final look in the final faces. Speak of it, boy-san. Speak about MK and... Speak.

Carlos, the man with sunglasses, talks as if he too has changed. He tells us how young men and women, lying in wait, exploded a black-market claymore on his platoon. The blast tore men to pieces, it hurled them high into the air; the human whirlwinds spun like stars, fell like rain. "Like rain they fell," says Carlos, mopping sweat from his brow. "Like rain."

Carlos says the CIA flew him to Florida. Doctors took nineteen steel fragments from his chest, eighteen from his face. He is blind. The CIA paid for medicine that stopped his nightmares, thoughts of killing himself; but then the gringos said, 'Now you must go.' He asked to stay, but they would not listen.

The Captain flares his elbow out, inclines his wrist, looks at his watch. "We have been here three hours," he says. "Perhaps we are done."

The Contras and the Americans, stand up. As is the custom, the room fills with the sound of our hearty applause.

We linger as the trio step from the stage. They are smiling merciless survivors. I try to speak, but no words come out.

The Captain looks my way, draws near. He double taps a packet of cigarettes against the edge of his palm, angles the pack up, snares a white, unfiltered stick by the touch of his mouth, tilts the pack toward me. I want to talk. I can't talk...

"No thanks," I say.

He reaches into his shirt pocket, plucks out a matchbook, opens it, closes it, strikes a match against the flint. *Snap*. The expanding orange flame illuminates the angular contours of his Latino face. The Captain lights the cigarette, blows the dying match out, lets it fall to the floor, snuffs it with his boot heel. The crackling tobacco recedes backwards as he floods his lungs with smoke, issues a blue gray plume.

"What is your name?" he asks.

The scent of his sweat bridges the gulf between us.

"Robert," I say.

"Roberto," he says, repeating the three-syllable word as if it were the last lines of a hero's elegiac poem, or the first lines of a country's private prayer. As if the man lay on a battlefield wounded, or was long dead, or had simply vanished. I don't know. All I know is that this man has set and survived ambushes, rocket and mortar attacks; has entered peaceful towns, bound the innocent, shot or raped the women, castrated the men, or with quick-flashing machete, amputated arms, legs, hands, breasts. Yet this murdering man, who cries out for a son, wife, lover, begins to shake, tremble, then weep, as he staggers into the arc of my medic's arms, which console

110

him. "You'll be alright," I whisper. "You'll be alright."

I absorb his racking sobs, brace his body with my own, speak to him in his language. *"Tranquilo, commandante. Tranquilo. Soy aqui por usted."*

"Easy, easy. I'm here for you," my dream self says.

"Disculpeme. Dispenseme. Soy un hombre malo...Una assassino. He cometido muchas maldades. A los mujeres, a los hombres, a los muchachos. Por que? Para la poder. Si...Si...He hecho el trabajo del diablo. Disculpeme, por favor..."

Margaret's tremulous voice tenders his words. "Forgive me. I am a bad man. I have done the devils work... killed people...for money...power...forgive me..."

After a silence, I open my wet eyes. The boy and Carlos flank me. They are bewildered, upset. Their battlefield commander has lost control. They have never seen him like this. Suddenly the boy lunges, grabs the officer by the throat, tears him away from me, slaps the weeping man across the face. *Slap. Slap. Slap.* The Captain reflexively buries his head in the wing of his arm, takes a long, measured breath. Straightening up, a cold blank look settles over his face. That is what the boy and Carlos want. That is how they survive.

The boy unlocks the door, opens it just enough for the Contras to slink out. In the bright tropic heat, they move like foxes, hunting or being hunted, it's hard to tell. A moment later, they vanish into the twisted rubble of Bluefields. There is nothing to say, so we remain silent.

On the return ride down river, we gringos sit mute, listening to the intermittent heart beat slap of the weathered prow against the whirling water; the continuous roar of the powerful engines. There is a bitter-sweet comfort in the rock and sway of the boat. Our time in Bluefields is done. We have worked hard, we have seen how others live, we have lived outside ourselves. Even so, from this day and for the rest of our journey, the Americans will look at me strangely. I have power and they know it. Without firing a single shot or loosening a stuttering burst on full automatic, without calling in pummeling air strikes or ground shaking-artillery, without laying unmerciful siege to pastoral landscapes, without filling the abundant sky with black scars of smoke, curling fingers of fire, without setting off the unbearable chant of unbearable screaming, without taking or tormenting willing or unwilling captives, I know evil and they fear it.

MK, maybe it's time to return our dead, their dead, all our wounds and wounded. And they may forgive us.

The POWs

The last time I saw Glenn he was humping the gun in our platoon. After so many years it wouldn't be easy. I imagined he might feel the same. I didn't know what to expect. At the first knock I rushed to the door. An old man, still handsome, but without his love bead necklace, or grimy boonie hat, or faded Cav patch on his fatigue shirt, weaponless, stood in the doorway.

The day we met I hadn't been in country more than a week. On a hot, dusty firebase, Skinner pointed to a handsome soldier walking toward us. "That's Sgt. Green," he said. "You see the scar? He humped the sixty until he got hit. He's good people. Know what I mean?" The three of us found an empty bunker, shared an opium laced joint. Exhaling a white plume, Glenn spoke of his home town, the women he'd slept with, the day he was shot.

"In and out, Doc," he said, patting his bicep. "In and out. Just like sex."

We laughed loud that night. On New Year's, during the ambush, Skinner tossed grenades, Glenn fired his M16 until the barrel glowed red. In April, he killed the wounded girl as she swung her AK at me. In June, after a nervous door gunner shot Johnny B, Glenn and I dragged the poor bastard down to a crater. These things raced through my mind as we embraced.

"Kate," said Glenn. "This is Doc. He was the medic." "Doc, this is my wife."

A slender woman, with long dark hair, large brown eyes, a loving smile, when Kate stepped forward I felt myself surrender into the arc of her arms. What was it about her? I have known so many women, and known so little love.

"Come in, come in," I managed to say.

The three of us sat in my living room, the walls of which, except for a large framed photo, are bare. I drew the blinds, opened the windows, turned up the lights. Glenn and Kate sat on the sofa; I sat on the wood bench.

"Cozy place you got here," said Glenn.

Kate's eyes wandered across the empty walls. Whatever she felt, she did not say.

"Which one are you, honey?" she asked, pointing to the platoon just back from patrol.

Our eyes are vacant. We are tired and thirsty and still shocked out. Redding the FNG had just been shot.

"Third from the left," said Glenn. "That's Doc, standing next to me."

Kate knew of the bunker rats that crawled over us at night. Knew that Glenn and I shared food, water, ammo, that I tended his cuts and scratches. There were things he never talked about.

"You look so young," said Kate. "And so tired. What happened? Were you..."

"How long was the drive?" I interrupted.

"Six hours," said Glenn, taking the cue. "Been here long, Doc?"

It began when I first saw NVA on the streets of Hanoi. It began at the haunting hush of the rubber plantation near the town of An Loc. It happened in Sumatra while walking a rain forest trail at dawn. It reared up at the visible cries of a thousand caged birds in a hundred markets around the world. I want to tell Glenn and Kate that after nine months I didn't know who or when or where I was and once home moved twelve times in two years before settling down.

"After travels in Asia I moved here in 2002."

"You went back?!" asked Glenn, as if the country is still a poisoned thing.

"Yes, it was a good trip, but...what about you guys? How did you meet?"

Kate looked at her husband, gently squeezed his hand, then told the story. In nursing school he was a rascal, she said. He drank and partied. He slept around.

"None of the female students trusted him!" she said, and pinched Glenn lovingly. Kate ignored him but after six months they dated. That was twenty-five years ago. "We both work in ER," said Glenn. "I like it. Never standing still or sitting down."

Kate put her hand on Glenn's shoulder. "We're so lucky," she said. "We love our work. We have everything we need." She tugged Glenn's good arm. "Don't we honey?!"

Not long after, we made plans for the day.

"Time to move out," said Glenn.

We drove into town, walked the cobblestone streets, peered in the windows of rustic shops, visited the bronze fisherman's statue overlooking the harbor. While Kate read the names of men lost at sea, Glenn took photographs. The wind gusted the waves choppy and white.

"Closer," he said

"Like this, honey?" asked Kate." She blew him a kiss, then tenderly put her arm around my waist.

"Smile, Doc. C'mon, smile," said Glenn. I try, and he peers, steps back, takes the goddamn picture. He saw it. The sad mournful heated look which I have never quite defeated.

At the shipyard, the scent of fuel and creosote hang thick in the air. A half-dozen trawlers, held aloft on a web of stilts, look like fish out of water. Beneath the boats, helmeted men with acetylene torches blister paint off hulls; captains and deck hands mend torn plastic nets. Thirty minutes later we drive to a pier side restaurant; weather beaten buoys and lobster traps hang from the walls. Kate and Glenn are beguiled by the varied shapes and colors.

"We don't have anything like that where we live," said Kate. She pointed toward the settling ocean. "It's so beautiful here."

We eat and make small talk, but the three of us know things are not right.

At the mile long beach, we doff our shoes and walk the shore line, Glenn and Kate holding hands. Nervous sandpipers scurry between the retreating waves. Excited dogs race into the water after well thrown frisbees. Circling gulls screech and caw. Behind us, in the grassy dunes, I swear that thin young men with jet black hair lay in wait. Kate is shivering. The wind off the water makes the fall air sting. Heading back to the car, Glenn holds her close. In my cramped kitchen, we look at the photographs Glenn has brought. One by one, I name the wounded and dead. My voice quivers when recalling the night sappers overran the base.

"Whenever Glenn takes out the photos you sent, he cries too," said Kate.

Glenn looks at me, then turns away.

"You all right?" I ask.

In a sharp tone, he says not to worry. He says I always worried too much. Then Glenn began to pace.

"What's wrong, brother?"

"Nothing, Doc. It don't mean nothing."

What I say next just spills out. "Skinner lives in Vermont. He keeps a pistol in every room in the house. He says he knows that's fucked up. He says..." I look at Kate. "Sorry 'bout that."

"Oh, Glenn has guns and he talks that way too."

"One in the car. Three in the house. Permit to carry. Got to protect yourself at all times, Doc," says Glenn. "Know what I mean? But that has nothing to do with Vietnam."

We thought they were dead. When the woman ran, we shot and missed. Skinner tossed a grenade. She was breathing when we found her. The look in her eyes. The long pleading look.

Glenn quickened his pace. It was my fault. Telling him it

would be good to meet. What can I do to make things right?

"You might like this," I say, adjusting the CD player. "It's called Gymnopedie."

Glenn asked what that meant. I said I don't know. No one does. I said this song calms me when nothing else works.

A minute into the melody, Glenn settled into Kate's arms as they sat on the couch. I turned the lights low. It was dark out when Glenn woke up.

"We ought to be going, honey," said Kate. "It's a long drive home."

They gathered their things, put on their coats.

In the doorway, after a long embrace, Glenn whispered, "I love you, Doc."

"I love you too," I said, hugging him one last time. I stood in the darkness, listening to the soft crump of car doors opened and shut, the muted roar of the engine, the receding zoom as the car pulled away. That was six months ago. I've not heard from them since.

Walking With Mr. Muhammad

Our faces drip with sweat as we hike the slender overgrown path deep in the Sumatran rainforest. I love the dense forbidding undergrowth, the thick scrub, the serpentine gauntlet of exposed twisting roots. I love the slippery moss-covered rocks, the dragon-like toppled rotting trees. I love the jungles sweet organic scent, the thorny hanging vines, the muted sunlight filtering past clouds of leaves. For one week, six hours a day, I trek with Mr. Muhammad, a dark-skinned wiry young man who is my guide in this blue-green paradise.

A hundred times, like Timmy Day, he lifts the well-honed machete up, brings it down, whack, whack, whack. But this morning no thirsty leeches fall from trees. There is no ambush site. No crimson kill zone, no pungent enemy scent. Today there is only our rhythmic cadence as we bend and dip, carefully push off the slippery rocks, crawl under or over fallen trees, gently pull back the yielding saplings, wipe the sweat from our brows. Yet my body is tense, my right hand shaped to an unseen trigger.

From time to time Mr. Muhammad surveys the jungle floor, or the canopy above.

"Monkey," he whispers, and seconds later, high overhead, a troop of gray haired Macaques make jittery vocals as they swing and scamper and disappear.

"How did you do that?"

He is the sort of man who knows what to say and when to

118

say it. As we cross cold rushing streams, climb soft steep hills, grab leathery tree trunks and rope-like roots to pull ourselves through muck and grime, as we plod and trudge past spiraling banyan trees, past emerald grooves of lush bamboo, deftly jog down narrow paths, I wonder if he knows what I'm feeling.

Two hours later, breathing hard, covered with dirt and sweat, we stop to rest. Mr. Muhammad peers and points to a half-hidden den thirty meters away.

"Tiger," he says, eyeing the empty lair. "Maybe he dead."

For an instant I relive the ritual: We walk into them. They walk into us. We walk into each other. During the firefight or ambush or rocket or mortar attack there are shouts and screams, the bleeding men call, "Medic!" Then choppers arrive for the wounded and dead, and quiet, so quiet, until it starts all over again.

"Wait here," says Mr. Muhammad, who melts into the jungle to cut and carve spears.

I lean forward, press my palms to my knees, shift an invisible ruck on my back, gulp down air. Suddenly, there is blood in my face, there is sadness and sorrow. I was the medic. Always, I ran or crawled forward whenever they shouted my name. "You'll be alright," I always said. I'm crying and hope that Mr. Muhammad does not hear or see it.

"For you," he says, stepping out of the jungle, and hands me a long pole tipped with a razor-sharp point. "You see tiger, you kill!" he laughs, and jabs his spear into the air.

I grip the weapon tightly, and we move out. But today is a good day. After an hour of hard trekking Mr. Muhammad says, "No tiger. Maybe he dead." Not far from our camp we pass the old woman in rags who lives with birds and cats in her rickety hut. Waving both hands, she grins and cackles.

"What happened to her?"

"She crazy."

Inside our snug cabin, Mr. Muhammad prepares Nasi Goreng. He mixes water, spices, eggs and rice in a large blackened pot. He strikes a match, lights a handful of tinder, gently blows until the embers catch and he builds up the fire with twigs and branches.

"From where you know jungle?" he asks as he stirs the food in widening circles.

There is the sizzle and crackling of burning wood. The comforting scrape of wood on metal. There is the sight and smell of rising steam that permeates the cabin with its fragrant scent. Soon the boiling rice erupts with miniature craters. The egg yolk curdles into delicate strips. Mr. Muhammad adds more cooking oil.

"Yes?" he asks, continuing to stir.

At the slightest sound we dropped to the earth, our helmets seeming to spin in the air. Then land mines exploded, or mortars rained down, or bullets whizzed and stung, and men became animals who screamed and shouted, as they fired their weapons, and cursed or called, and then like magic, it suddenly stopped.

My guide scoops equal portions of the rust-colored meal onto two metal plates. He asks again, and my answering voice is loud and harsh, and I don't know what I'm saying or how long I say it, but at the touch of his hand I grow quiet.

After we finish the meal, after Mr. Muhammad has cleaned the pot and plates and puts out the fire, he lays out two straw mats and coarse cotton blankets on the wood plank floor. Calmly, he takes the bed on the right.

"You must sleep," he says, "Sleep."

Night

7 July 1980

I'm in a large empty house. My brother and I are dressed like soldiers. We're hunting each other down. I see him before he spots me and hit him with a burst from my M-16. I walk the bullets up to him, but they make only small BB holes. There's little noise or impact, but he falls and I rush to his aid. I feel sorry for him, for what I have done.

28 June 1999

I'm with a group of people in danger. A seated black woman, who is light-skinned, over and over repeats, "If ever I go. If ever I go." She's unaware that she's dying. I take her in my arms to divert her attention. I imagine a man from behind will execute her. At the last moment I will say, "Never mind. Shoot us both."

19 January 2000

I'm at Pine Grove sleep away camp preparing for war. Low flying jets fire rockets into the distance. We cheer as the missiles whoosh and spiral to their targets. We move out, juvenile soldiers, all less than fifteen. In a large field teenage soldiers explode a device that releases a smoky fog that appears to be toxic. At detonation I'm hit by shrapnel. I feel the cardboard splinters penetrate my back, but they do me no harm.

We march back to our starting point. I'm walking uphill on the wide trail which leads from the lake to the bunk houses, weary from the weight of my pack. I walk next to an out-of-shape youngster. He huffs and puffs. In his hand he carries a silver-plated toy luger.

26 January 2000

I'm a guest renting a room in a residential area filled with many large wood houses. I'm skateboarding down a narrow sidewalk, propelling the board by clenching my toes and pushing down hard. The people are friendly. A block away a tree catches fire. A fierce wind blows the flames out of control. The sky turns white from heat. The house where I'm staying may catch fire. No one panics. I rush inside to recover my pack but I'm lost and can't tell which room is mine. I look about. My things are missing. I find them in a room with no back wall. On the way out I watch an attractive woman undress. Outside everyone is calm. I meet a young veterinarian. His dog, burned on its back and aware of its wounds remains feisty. Humorously I say to the doctor, "So, you have casualties." He is optimistic.

4 February 2001

I'm with a large black woman who resembles the poet Marilyn Nelson. We're sitting in the office of Dr Ahr. She listens while I speak about war. Suddenly a low resonant howl escapes me. The black woman says, "I know what that is." I begin weeping.

17 February 2001

On a cancer ward all of the patients are men. One complains that his nose is too large. Another declares that without his doctor he would have died, but has lived an extra two years. The ward is home-like. The doctors are friendly. Each has his own cure; some succeed, others fail. My doctor is a woman. She is dedicated and loving.

A staff member and I reach a doctor's office at the same time. I push the door open; it's immediately slammed shut. The staff member knocks and is let in. I leave, aware that protocol must be obeyed.

I become frustrated and rebel. For punishment I'm sent to a large forest to gather pine needles in long neat rows. After several hours on my hands and knees I try to escape. Using a dog, my doctor captures me. I quit the ward. In her presence I get dressed. I'll be traveling heavy–there are my two backpacks, a toothbrush too small for my mouth. My doctor tries to discourage me, but I'm angry and sad. On the wall hangs a photograph of a male doctor at war. His pants are torn and dirty. His knees are wounded; he's running for help. I say, "What does he know? I was the medic. They all came to me." I begin weeping.

2 July 2001

I'm in a large room at ground level. Its green walls and floors are made of smoothed out earth. Large square windows without glass overlook a forbidding no-man's-land. The NVA begin shooting. I return fire. They're everywhere. Several reach in. I push them off and continue shooting. They are everywhere but I'm not afraid. I keep fighting. There is no escape.

25 July 2001

I'm brought back to Vietnam. The platoon tells me I look good. I'm wearing my old jungle fatigues and steel helmet. I have no weapon, no gear, no leech straps beneath my knees. I want to tell them that dressed like this, ordinary people think I'm strange, but I keep silent.

Mike and I walk to the water point. We pass through a small town, then into forest where I become lost. I walk to a highway, then pass through a circle of college students. I expect unkind remarks, but the students are friendly.

At a busy traffic intersection a college professor smiles.

"Where's the water?" I ask. He tells me. I find a dark, turbulent river. This can't be the water point, though I know it is. Frustrated I sleep under a moon lit canopy of thick brush. I wake up under a large plastic tarp. Crawling forward I accidentally wake the lieutenant. I say, "It's me, Doc." He throws me a pair of bowling shoes that are too small. A man I've never seen glares at me with contempt, then throws me a pair that fit. Then everyone leaves. I look out from beneath the tarp. Someone inside a nearby house appears in silhouette, then vanishes. I anticipate an ambush. I imagine being shot in the head. I imagine how the lieutenant will comfort me. It's raining. I have no water, ammo, or weapon.

14 September 2001

I'm with my old platoon on LZ Ranch in Cambodia. We're pressed up against the berm. An attack is coming. My M-16 is broken. There's no trigger or clip. A sergeant offers me his weapon, but I refuse, saying he is the better grunt.

The scene changes. We're in a village. An old VC hides in a hut hoping to escape. I throw him down and sit on him. He's taken prisoner, but will not speak. I devise a way to torture him. We dig a vertical hole, bury him up to his neck, then place a clear plastic cover over his head. We urinate on him, but the VC is stubborn and stays silent. He accepts that he will die.

We hear shooting and rush for cover. I find a Viet Cong who resembles David Boyle, my college best friend. He tries to steal American weapons from a display case, but instead, grabs an umbrella. I tell him to give up. When he refuses, we fight. Each time I stab his belly he says, "Kill me." I feel terrible. It's as if I knew this man. When he weakens I take him in my arms and call for help. His stomach leaks on me. I'm crying. I'm saying "Oh God...Oh God," American soldiers arrive. They look perplexed, awed. We march to the hospital.[1]

1 July 2002

A young soldier shows me a gem bought from a villager. He regards its beauty and power but I can tell it's fake. The villager, who is middle aged and wears a business suit, leaves his house. He walks toward me. I throw the gem in his face.

"What are you doing?" I say. "This is uranium." Aloof and calm, he curls his hand around my neck then releases it. We return to his house. There is the long flight home. I begin planning my escape.

9 July 2002

I'm on a combat assault. Only a few of us ride in the chopper. Most stand on the slicks. We carry full combat gear: pack, weapon, ammo. We fly toward the Ivy Hill Apartments. From high up I see buildings, which appear like photographs. We land on a roof top. I see my brother. At the same time, I see a terrible sight and walk toward it. The intact body of an American soldier glows like fireplace embers. His internal organs, hardened to stone, are fully visible. I shout to my brother, "How did this happen?" He says he doesn't know. I can tell my brother is lying.

---

[1] In 1994 the author met and worked with Dr. Jamie Harter and his wife, Dr. Sue Girod, at Southland Hospital in Invercargill, New Zealand. By an odd coincidence, both doctors knew Stevie Sharp, the author's platoon leader in Vietnam, who had become the sheriff of their home town, Bloomington, Indiana. In 2001 the author stayed at their home, where the above dream occurred after visiting Sheriff Sharp.

Maryann

Martin saw the ad in a magazine, plucked from one of several tin boxes chained, 'handcuffed,' he had said to himself, to a traffic light on 7th Ave. He was in the habit of reading them, and kept a stack of fresh one dollar bills in a desk drawer. *'Insert your response in an envelope. Do not seal it. Put the box number you are responding to on the front of the envelope. Put a stamp on the envelope. Now place the envelope and two dollars into a second envelope. Seal the second envelope. Address it to Sity Singles, PO Box 4041 Ansonia Station, New York, NY 10025. Make sure you have placed sufficient postage on the second envelope. For multiple responses, repeat the above.'*

Martin was forty-four years old and straight but he read them all. Women seeking Men, Men seeking Men, Women seeking Women, Couples, Anything Goes. Afterwards, he would return to the straight section. On a good day he would think to himself, well, you never know. Bad days he was less positive about himself. He scanned.

"SWF, 40's, attractive, well-traveled, successful, outgoing, literate, enjoys Bach to Bon Jovi, museums, art, theater, culture, seeks honest, caring, successful man for committed relationship. Note, photo, phone."

Too much for me to handle, he thought, and continued to finger down the line. The uncommon epithets, those with wit or clever word plays sometimes made him laugh. Most often it was the odd or eccentric that attracted him. His favorite was, "Yeah, yea, I know the drill. I am woman, I am strong. Lonely SJF 46, seeks nice guy to fill a bowl of chicken soup for. Be sane and interesting. Got a job? Great! Let's meet!'

He thought of writing her, but the ad had disappeared the following month. Martin felt he had missed the opportunity of a life time.

'So far so bad,' he said to the lead painted walls. In five months he had moved six times since returning from a year's travel in Asia and Europe. Depressed and fragmented in the cramped and stuffy $300 a month YMCA room, he realized it was the same as '92, when he had traveled in Central America for several months. It had taken him a year to readjust. How was it that he could leave and travel, occasionally find himself in good company for extended periods of time, then come back and *crash and burn*. Where had he heard the phrase? From a chopper pilot. After the war.

"Good news, Aquarius. Your moon is in transit with Mercury. This is a good time to invest in stocks and bonds. Or buy that new 4x4 Rover you've been eyeing. Your special powers of imagination are now working for you, Aquarius. This is a great time to communicate your innovative ideas to those special persons around you."

Martin settled back onto the dismal foam bed and laughed thru the haze of his anxiety. "Who you kidding, man?" he said to the four plaster walls and brown wooden floor. The words echoed off the rusted footlocker two feet from his head. Outside, in the firetrap hallway, someone shouted street directions into the pay phone.

"Left, bitch. Two blocks south, then hang a damn right. You got that? Bitch! Hoe! You got it?" It was Larry the crack head speaking to his girlfriend.

The phone slammed down hard. A moment later coins dropped into the machine; a deep voice spoke softly, perhaps to a wife. There were fifteen transient men on the floor. After six weeks Martin had grown used to the human parade.

He turned the page and continued down the list of Women seeking Men, reading just the first line of each ad.

"Let me be the chocolate icing on your thick fudge cake!"

"SWF Vegan sex goddess seeks thick hunk of dark meat."

"SWCFNS seeks Clint Eastwood look-alike with Richard Nixon values for LTR."

He smirked. They were hilarious, they flowed like poems, and took his mind off himself.

"The chocolate icing on your thick fudge cake," he mouthed, and tasted the word play.

Outside, Martin recognized the shuffle step of Jeremy the ex-Marine, intent on his evening toilette. Sixty pounds overweight, a chain smoker, the USMC bulldog tattoo still visible on his bloated arm, Jeremy collected welfare, visited his parole officer twice weekly.

Once Martin heard Jeremy talk to himself in front of the cracked mirrors over the communal sinks.

"Good looking corpse...gonna make a good-looking corpse..." he repeated over and over. He had fought in Korea. He drank.

Martin wanted to speak to him, another vet. Jeremy kept to himself.

Fucking Marines, Martin thought. The Cav saved your ass beaucoup times.

"Sexy Senior seeks gentleman for the company of his pleasure.."

"People say I have a lot to give but I give to much of myself."

Martin read on. About women in search of white knights, about candle lit dinners and all life has to offer, ballet, sailing, opera, must like cats, mensch, hot times, unslim; then ran his finger once more over the black and white column of babble.

"...the company of his pleasure. You will not be disappointed."

He put the paper down, closed his eyes, recalled past encounters. Judy had written back immediately, eager to meet him, once out of prison.

"The police pulled me over because of a broken tail light. When they opened the hood they found ten kilos. But it wasn't mine. Honest. Anyway, I'll be getting out soon and would really like to meet you, Martin. You sound SO interesting." He'd thrown the scented letter and soft porn photo into the garbage. Bonnie promised high heels and negligees. But when they spoke by phone she rattled off a list of unquaint conditions, including $200 each time they had sex. "Well, no thanks," Martin said. "That's your choice," she had countered. "Have a pleasant day," he rejoined, then hung up. Ann from Canada sent a computer generated letter, the dot matrix crotch shot poised over, "I *really* want to meet you, Martin Berry 1482 River Street, Tarrytown, New Jersey 10591 USA. But first I'd like you to see my very personal video, only $19.95 plus $4.95 for shipping and handling." He called the postal inspectors in both countries.

Once, three weeks before leaving the country for Central America, he wrote to a woman advertising in a literary magazine. "While the mouse is away the cat will play. Forties SWF has nine months alone while husband is on sabbatical. Seeking good lover." Martin expressed his desire to make love slowly; foreplay was most important. He had a fondness for standing in front of full length mirrors and undressing women while he stood behind. I'll raise your skirt up and enter you, your breasts cupped in my hands. Would you like that? I'll kiss you everywhere. Where do you liked to be kissed? Afterwards, when we're spent, I'll kiss you to sleep. He sent off the note and forgot about it.

Her reply came ten days after the plane tickets for Guatemala arrived.

"Dear Martin,

Of the forty-one responses I received, yours was the only one that was straightforward and to the point. I too enjoy lovemaking standing up, but seated as well, and standing face to face, and in the bath. Martin, I would love to see you. Please call me soon to arrange our first meeting."

He wondered what to do. Stay, and lose the chance to travel? She seemed sincere. He wrote her the truth and departed a week later.

Martin carefully circled the oblong box. Sexy Senior. She can't be that old, he reassured himself.

Maryann called a week later. Her voice reminded him of cake sales and hand knitted sweaters. They made small talk, chatted about the weather, music, their likes and dislikes, her garden, his travels.

"And what kind of work do you do, dear? To go to all those places?"

"Well, I get a pension from the Veterans Administration."

"A government pension? Goodness! Were you wounded badly?"

"Yes," he lied.

"But you can, well, you know..."

"Make love?" Martin said to the older woman.

"Not that I..."

"Yes," he said, "I can do that."

There was a momentary pause.

"You're certainly welcome to drop by," she said flawlessly.

"I'd like to," said Martin, as calmly as possible.

"Three o'clock on the 20th?" she asked. "You can take a cab from the train station in Crestwood. I'll pay for it, dear."

"Sure," he said. "I'll see you then." He gently hung up the phone.

Well, what have I got to lose? he thought. She can't be *that* old.

Martin worked out extra hard for a week. Stretching and calisthenics. His body was trim. He weighed one hundred and fifty-five pounds. Afterwards, he would look at the war photo of himself taped to the wall. He could see no difference

130

between then and now. It was a good shot, taken on patrol somewhere in Tay Ninh. He stood bent slightly forward, head tilted up, straining under the weight of his helmet and pack. The M-16 hung sideways, a stiff metal flag draped across his chest over three bandoliers of ammo, his aid bag, the forty-five, his canteens of water, the fragmentation grenades. He hadn't smiled, but looked directly into the camera, the angular features shock set and weary.

"Say cheese," the point man said.

But he hadn't and they were ambushed soon after. And Bill Williams was dead. When Martin looked at the photo he sobbed.

Pools of sweat glistened on the wooden floor. Even the window had fogged up. He stepped out to shower, face flushed, sweat streaming off his body from exercise in the cubicle room.

"What you been up to, man?" Larry whined.

Martin looked directly at the pitiful human being; the endorphins always burnt a pleasant hole thru his private agony.

"Fucking," he said, dead serious. "I be fucking."

The communal shower was empty. The cold water felt good on his head and body.

"You's a sick motherfucker, old man," the young addict shouted. "Sick..sick..sick."

The shrill voice echoed and drowned in the chip tiled chamber. Martin grinned. The words rolled playfully off his tongue.

"The chocolate icing on your thick fudge cake."

He stepped out of the shower, toweled down, brushed his teeth. Why was he doing this? he wondered, though he secretly knew. Depressed, anxious, Martin saw himself incapable of all but the simplest of causal encounters. Besides, since the war it had always been this way. Only now the government gave him money for PTSD. He recalled the exam thru the fractured mirror.

"All I know, I went back to Viet Nam last year and something snapped."

The psychiatrist had nodded curtly, raised his eye brows with muted concern. Martin burst into tears for the rest of the hour.

Well, he thought, at least it's a start. As far as he could tell, she lived a few towns over, had money, and they were both discreetly horny.

He took the train from Grand Central, got off at Crestwood, walked down to the stationary store, bought a scratch off lottery ticket, won three dollars and hailed a cab.

"32 Lincoln Lane," he told the driver," his voice uplifted. "Where you from, man?"

"Haiti," the cabbie said. The whites of his eyes flashed in the rearview mirror, the afternoon sun absorbed into dark brown skin.

"Haiti," Martin said. 'You come over here before or after Papa Doc?"

"Ahhh. I left in the time of Baby Doc, my friend. It was hard. Very bad. I am here now many years. I have a house, my wife, children; the taxi, she's mine. For me that is enough. And you? From Crestwood? I haven't seen you before."

"Tarrytown," Martin said. "Just visiting a friend."

"She's nice in Tarrytown, yes?"

"Can't complain. And Crestwood?"

"Oh, Crestwood she's very nice, indeed. What number did you say?"

Martin looked out the window at the manicured lawns, the unfenced yards, the well-kept Tudor and neo colonial homes; felt the wealthy sway of the road.

"Thirty-two," he said.

"Yes, my friend. Twenty-eight, thirty...thirty two she is."

The driver glided to the curb of a large house with a red painted door.

"Here," Martin said, stepping out before the man could

give him change.

"Have a good afternoon," he said, and snapped the door smartly shut.

"Yessss, a good afternoon," the driver said. He eyed the three-dollar tip, then sped off.

Maryann looked remarkably like the mother of a friend from college, which, he calculated, would make her roughly sixty-four. She *was* old. They sat at her living room table.

"Not too long," Martin said, in answer to how long the trip had taken.

He noted her bronze tinted hair, the over rouged cheeks, liver-spotted hands, the deep wrinkled lines of her face. Yet beneath the blue silk blouse, her intriguing breasts. She was not very pretty, he thought, but at least...

Martin had not slept with a woman in nearly two years. He imagined how he would unbutton her, take the delicate cups into his hands and mouth. He would close his eyes, suckle long and hard, recall other women, unfasten his pants, penetrate her like he had not done in so long. He suddenly recalled the Columbian prostitute in Amsterdam, where he first 'crashed and burned' on the way home from his travels in Southeast Asia. They conversed in Spanish. About the price, what he wanted, and didn't: SIDA. He spoke to her easily, without shame. "I want sex first. Afterwards, will you let me hold you? Will you hold me? That's all I want." She undressed, set her clothes on the back of a wooden chair, filled a plastic bowl with warm water; placed a yellow towel nearby. Afterward, she let him fall asleep in her arms. His head spun less for hours.

Maryann said, "Let me show you..." She gestured to the rest of her home.

"The bedroom?" Martin said, surprising himself.

"Why, I hadn't really thought of that, dear, but, oh, why not?" she feigned.

She offered her hand; he led her upstairs to the second

floor of the spacious house.

"It's the second door on the left, dear."

They undressed quickly.

"But why not?" Maryann said, looking from his limpness to her parted legs. "Why won't you do it? Honestly, dear. I thought... Don't you like doing that?"

Martin looked at her splayed naked on the double bed. Spindle legged, her belly a cummerbund of fat, it was one thing to sit in the company of this older woman, quite another to...still, she had well proportioned, near Venus de Milo breasts. And it had been so fuckin' long.

Maryann rose up, touched him, drew him near. For several minutes he lay with her, not moving. She stroked the back of his neck. How did she know? That's all I want, old woman. Just keep doing that. I'll pay you. How much? Thirty guilders? Alright, alright, we'll do it, for God's sake. I'll probably explode. Let me hold you. Hold me. Hold me. That's all I want.

She grew restless, trailed her finger tips up and down the length of his cock.

"Oh dear, oh dear," Maryann said, fondling his splendid erection. "Martin, please."

Martin paused to collect his thoughts, to dilute the anguish of his reply. She really *is* old, he thought, and looked at the white and grey spangled stubble brooding between her legs. In college the girls called him 'Mr. Hips' in awe of his churning loins. He had learned the technique on R&R.

"Can you, well, help me," he said to the young prostitute in Japan.

"I've just come out of combat. I'm not sure I can, you know...do it."

She smiled, unzipped her black cocktail dress, removed her long-haired wig, counted his 30,000 yen, rapidly circled her hips clockwise, then counter clockwise; ground his virginity to pulp.

"GI, Me goo fuck," she yawned.

He took a photo of her while she slept. The college girls went wild whenever he duplicated her technical sex.

Martin looked at Maryann. Not in a million years, baby. Not in a million fuckin years. Still, her breasts were beautiful. Oh Christ. He lay down next to her. It had been too long.

"Please, Martin, dear. Goodness, look how big you are. Don't you want to make love to me?"

"Like this?" Martin said.

With startling ease he entered her, closed his eyes, performed.

They awoke two hours later. He thought of the time it would take to return home. Cab. Train. Walk up the hill. Go to the Chinese take-out next to the VFW hall. He would give them money.

"Buddhist Delight," he would say.

They would give him food.

"Goodness, it's late," Maryann said. "Are you hungry dear, I can fix you something to eat."

She began to dress.

"Not yet," said Martin. He pulled her down beside him, nestled his head between her breasts, suckled ravenously, then softly kissed the perfect nipples, the aromatic cleavage.

"Oh, Martin, dear, it's 10 o'clock. I have work tomorrow. And I have to take my pills, you know. Can we make it another time? Shall we?" She slipped forty dollars on the night table. The sight of it made him uneasy.

"I'll call a cab," Martin said, letting her go.

In the lamp light he imagined she was good looking in her youth.

"You'll call me next week, dear?"

"Yes," Martin said. He put on his coat.

Maryann hugged him before he walked out the door.

"Goodness, wherever did you learn to do it like that?"

He felt her frailness push up against him. Was she reliving her youth? She was old enough to be...he would not admit it.

He had fucked her, and fallen asleep in her arms.

"The cab's here," he said. Eyes closed, he kissed her on the cheek.

"Get home safe, dear. Have a safe trip."

"Four dollah," the Chinese girl said, handing him the order.

"Chopstick?" he said. She always forgot.

"Soy Sauce?"

"Just one, please."

She tossed in three, plus a thimble of Hot and Spicy Mustard and two of the sticky goo Duck Sauce. It was their nightly ritual.

"Good night," said Martin.

"Goo night, mistah," she always replied.

He went immediately to his room, wolfed the food down, slurped water from a cold-water faucet in the bathroom, brushed his teeth, lay down on the foam bed, clicked the overhead light switch off and drifted to uneasy sleep.

Attributions

"Speak Out." First published in *Will Work for Peace*. Zeropanik Press, 1999. Subsequently filmed in *The Real Deal*, distributed by The Cinema Guild, 2000.

"How Stevie Nearly Lost the War." First published in *New Millennium Writings 2004-2005*, Issue 14. Subsequently published in *More Than a Memory: Reflections of Viet Nam*. Modern History Press, 2008.

"Off the Road." First published in *Places Magazine*, Spring 2002. Subsequently published in *More Than a Memory: Reflections of Viet Nam*. Modern History Press, 2008.

"Torque At Angkor Wat." First published in *Slowtrains.com*, Fall 2005. Subsequently published in *More Than a Memory: Reflections of Viet Nam*. Modern History Press, 2008.

"When He Was Good." First published in *Suspect Thoughts.com*, 2001. Subsequently published in *The Mammoth Book of Best New Erotica*. Carroll & Graf, 2001.

"The Exit Stage." First published in *Slowtrains.com*, Fall 2003. Subsequently published in *Bi Guys, First Hand Fiction for Bisexual Men and Their Admirers*. Hawthorn Press, 2006.

"After Reaching the Home of Juan Pablo Lorenz." First published in *ChamberFour.com* in February 2011.

"Walking With Mr. Muhammad." First published in *counterpunch.org* in November 2009.

"Bluefields." First published in *Cutthroat*, Volume 2, Number 1, Spring 2007.

"Maryann." First published in *Cleansheets.com* in February 1999. Subsequently published in *The Unmade Bed*. Masquerade Books, August 1999. And in *Best New American Erotica 2000*. Simon & Schuster, 2000.

"Night." First published as "Excerpts From A Dream Journal" in *So It Goes, The Literary Journal of The Kurt Vonnegut Museum *Library*, Issue 5, 2016.

Marc Levy was an infantry medic in D 1/7 First Cavalry in Vietnam/Cambodia in 1970. His decorations include the Silver Star, two Bronze Stars, the Air Medal and ArCom. His work has appeared in various publications including *New Millennium Writings, Cutthroat, Slant, War, Literature and the Arts, CounterPunch, Best American Erotica 2000, Mudfish, So It Goes, Stone Canoe, New Madrid* and VVA's *The Veteran.* It is forthcoming in VFP's *In Our Peace Times.* He won the 2016 Syracuse University Institute for Veterans and Military Families Writing Prize, judged by Brian Turner.

email: silverspartan@gmail.com
website: MedicInTheGreenTime.com

.

48547223R00093

Made in the USA
Middletown, DE
21 September 2017